And One for All

YEARLING BOOKS are designed especially to entertain and enlighten young people. Patricia Reilly Giff, consultant to this series, received her bachelor's degree from Marymount College and a master's degree in history from St. John's University. She holds a Professional Diploma in Reading and a Doctorate of Humane Letters from Hofstra University. She was a teacher and reading consultant for many years, and is the author of numerous books for young readers.

For a complete listing of all Yearling titles, write to
Dell Readers Service, P.O. Box 1045,
South Holland, IL 60473.

AND ONE FOR ALL

THERESA NELSON

A Yearling Book

Published by
Bantam Doubleday Dell Books for Young Readers
a division of
Bantam Doubleday Dell Publishing Group, Inc.
1540 Broadway
New York, New York 10036

Acknowledgments

Staff Sergeant Peter Farrenkopf, Sergeant Glynis Harvey, Gunnery Sergeant
Smith, Staff Sergeant Grevious (all of the White Plains, New York, Marine
Recruiting Office)

ISBN: 0-440-40456-8

Reprinted by arrangement with Franklin Watts, Inc., on behalf of
Orchard Books

Printed in the United States of America

May 1991

10 9 8 7 6 5

OPM

For Daddy

And One for All

prologue

EASTER
1968

There were snakes in the cellar.

It was black as pitch down the back stairs, but Geraldine could see them anyway, staring up at her with their terrible eyes.

"Don't go down there, Wing!" she cried.

Wing was laughing. "What's the matter, Geriatric? They're dead, remember? Dead snakes never hurt anybody. Look, I'll show you—"

"No, Wing—stay away from the door—you'll fall!" But it was too late; he was falling already, and she was falling after him. She opened her mouth to cry out, but no sound came; she was falling, falling. . . .

The Trailways bus lurched over a pothole, and Geraldine gasped and jerked awake. She'd been sleeping in fits and starts ever since she left the White Plains terminal at six-thirty this morning.

"Are you all right, dear?" the woman next to her asked, looking up from her paperback romance.

"Yes, ma'am," Geraldine answered. "I guess I was just dreaming."

The woman nodded sympathetically, then added, "Your first trip to the capital?"

"Yes, ma'am. I mean, no—I was there once when I was little, but I don't remember it much." Geraldine's voice sounded strange in her own ears, as if it were coming from someone else.

"Well, you've picked a nice time to go back—I hope the cherry trees are in bloom! You must be sure to look for the cherry blossoms; they're always worth seeing."

"Yes, ma'am," Geraldine murmured. It was hard to believe that cherry blossoms could matter to anyone today. Would Sam be noticing the cherry blossoms? she wondered. Was that where she'd find him, walking down some sidewalk, laughing with his new friends, cherry petals drifting like snow around their heads? Involuntarily she shivered a little.

The woman gave her a keen look. "Are you sure you're all right?" she asked again.

"Yes, ma'am," Geraldine lied. "I'm fine."

The woman smiled. "You'll have to forgive me—I have a daughter about your age, thinks her mother is just an old worry wart. She'll be thirteen next month."

Geraldine noticed the two white spots on the woman's front teeth, the mole on her left cheek, the tiny laugh lines crinkled at the corners of her eyes. Brown eyes, brown as mud.

Like Wing's, Geraldine thought, with a sudden tightening in her throat.

When she was little—three or so—she had thought that it must be harder to see out of brown eyes, that light would have trouble getting through such a dark color. She once suggested to her mother that maybe that was why Wing had such a hard time with reading.

"No, honey," Mama answered, "it doesn't have anything to do with the color of his eyes." Her voice was tired; she had been sitting with Wing at the dining room table for more than an hour, listening to him struggle with his second-grade textbook.

"Rrr," Geraldine heard him saying, over and over, and then, "uh," and finally, "nnn."

"That's right, Wing," Mama encouraged him. "Rrr–uh–nnn; now, just put the sounds together—"

But Wing had hesitated, confused. Sweat began to form in bright beads along his upper lip. "Rrr," he began again, then paused, frowning.

"Run!" Geraldine piped up, trying to help. "Rrr–uh–nnn makes run!"

"That's right, baby," Mama said quietly, and Geraldine had felt proud, but Wing only scowled at her and bolted outside, muttering, "I *hate* school!" slamming the door behind him. And so Geraldine had made the suggestion about brown eyes. . . .

The woman was still smiling. "Are you visiting relatives in Washington?"

"No, ma'am," Geraldine heard herself say, and

then, since the woman was still waiting for more, she added, "Just a—a guy I know." She'd been about to say "a friend" but had caught herself in time. Sam wasn't her friend anymore.

The woman's eyebrows arched slightly. "I see. How nice," she said, but her voice had a disapproving edge to it. "He'll be meeting you at the station, then?"

Geraldine opened her mouth to say no, then changed her mind. "Yes, ma'am," she said, hoping that would satisfy her, though the truth was Sam had no idea she was following him to Washington.

"Well, that's good. No sense courting danger, is what I always tell Cindy. My daughter. You know how these big cities are—I can hardly open the paper without trembling, these days."

"Yes, ma'am." Geraldine nodded wearily. She was starting to feel like an idiot with all her *ma'am*ing, but she couldn't seem to stop herself. Mama cared so much for *ma'ams* and *sirs* that she'd fed them to the Brennan children with their teething biscuits.

"Of course, Cindy thinks I'm being silly, tells me she's old enough to take care of herself." The woman rolled her eyes at this idea. "That's the trouble with these New York City kids; they all think they're so tough, sophisticated—it just kills me. And then first thing you know, you turn on the television and there's been another mugging or murder—or even worse," she hinted darkly. "And of course now there's all this racial tension, too, since Dr. King's assassination. . . ." She shook her head. "Are you from New York?"

"No, ma'am." Another expectant pause. "From the country up north of it," Geraldine answered vaguely. "Near the reservoirs."

"Oh, I know that area well. I have a cousin who lives up that way. I just love the country—aren't you the lucky one, living there all the time?"

"Yes, ma'am," she said, and then without warning she was hit with a wave of homesickness for the old white house on the hill, of longing for Mama and Daddy and Wing and Dub and for Sam, too, the way he used to be; for everything, the way it used to be. She steeled herself until the feeling passed, called up in its place the coldness of what she was about to do, the image of Sam, laughing, blind to what he had done. Sam, walking beneath the cherry trees.

The woman looked as if she'd be glad to talk some more, but Geraldine didn't think she could manage it, just now. She turned away and leaned her forehead against the cloudy windowpane, stared out at the unfamiliar landscape rushing by. She felt heavy, dull with fatigue. Don't sleep anymore, she told herself; we'll be there soon. But her eyes closed, and in her mind the cellar gaped, black and full of snakes.

part one

1966

She hated those stupid snakes. They were dead, sure, but they were still awful—dead snakes floating in glass jars filled with formaldehyde, lined up in neat rows on the cellar shelves. Great Uncle Doyle, long dead himself now, had collected reptile specimens as a boy. That was why they were there.

"Can't we throw them out?" Mama asked Daddy time and again. She was from Texas, where they didn't have cellars, and didn't care much for snakes, either. Still, she felt she had to ask. The house and everything in it had been in Daddy's family for ages—used to be the seat of a prosperous farm before the Depression—and he was attached to all the old things. Even the snakes.

"No, no," he would protest, "don't throw them out! The children might be able to use them in school sometime." Daddy had a high regard for education—none higher—though he had never gone past eleventh grade himself.

And so there were snakes in the cellar.

"Hail-Mary-full-of-grace-the-Lord-is-with-thee...."
Geraldine mouthed the words silently as she descended the narrow stairs. She knew she was being silly, knew that twelve was too old for imagining that pickled snakes could harm her. But the prayer made her feel better all the same. Walking quickly, looking neither right nor left, she made a beeline for the washing machine and dryer which had just rattled to a halt. Mama had sent her down to see if the checkered tablecloth was dry yet. Company for supper tonight. Well, not company, exactly; Sam Daily and his mother were more like family. But Mama wanted everything to be nice. "One last celebration," she had said, "to mark the end of another fine summer, the beginning of another fine school year."

There was a sudden loud creaking sound from above, and Geraldine jumped and stifled a scream. "Wing?" she called suspiciously. "Is that you?" There was no answer. Stupid, she told herself, it's only Mama, walking around in the kitchen. But she glanced up nervously at the lone bare bulb—sixty-watt—hanging overhead.

Wing's favorite trick of all, his rottenest, most sure-fire method of getting Geraldine's goat, was to wait until she was down in the cellar, then flip the switch at the top of the stairs and slam the door shut, closing her inside. In the dark. With the snakes. It really burned her up when he did that. He was seventeen years old, for crying out loud, and ought to have outgrown such childish pranks, right? Fat chance. The light flickered—Geraldine was sure of it this time. She tensed like a cat, her heart racing. "Wing Brennan, I'm warning you—"

But nothing happened. Geraldine reached up and tapped the bulb. It sputtered again. She gave it a quick twist in the socket and scolded herself for being such a chicken—good grief, he has me right where he wants me. Without even lifting a finger! Sighing, she opened the dryer door, took out the tablecloth and the rest of the laundry, folded the lot, then tucked it all under her chin and spat out another Hail Mary through clenched teeth as she scooted once more past those fool snakes, up the cellar stairs.

Mama had been alone in the kitchen when Geraldine left it ten minutes ago, but it was chockful now— the whole gang was here except for Daddy, who was still at work: Mama, Geraldine's little brother Dub, Wing and Wing's fat black dog Kizzy, and the Dailys, who had just arrived—tall and smiling, both of them. Mrs. Daily was standing beside Mama at the sink, laughing about something or other. "Hello, Geraldine," she said, her clear eyes shining behind glasses, teacher-like. Which she was.

"Hi," said Geraldine, smiling back.

Sam was standing with Wing—towering over him, actually. Mutt and Jeff, people called the two of them, like those guys in the funny papers. "Hey, fella," he said to her.

"Hey, Sam."

Wing was grinning. "What was all that noise down

in the cellar just now, Geriatric?" he asked. One of his teachers last year had somehow got it through Wing's head that "geriatric" meant "old lady."

She blushed. "What noise?" she answered. "I didn't hear any noise." She didn't want Sam to know she had been hollering over nothing, jumping at shadows.

Sam. She had loved him almost as far back as she could remember—ever since the summer of 1960, when he and his mother first moved into the old DuBarry place, about a mile down the road from the Brennans. There wasn't any father. He'd been killed in Korea when Sam was two years old. Sam had been Wing's best friend from the day they met, the only best friend Wing had ever had, or cared to have. Wing did have *some* sense, after all. But then everybody loved Sam—you couldn't help it, really.

Wing shrugged. "Could've sworn I heard you yell," he went on. " 'Wing Brennan, I'm warning you—' " he mimicked in a voice like Minnie Mouse's.

She glared at him, but Sam grinned and said, "That's really nice, Brennan—you trying out for glee club this term?"

"Look what the Dailys have brought us, Geraldine," Mama said, holding up a bagful of green stuff. "Sweet corn from their garden—silver and gold, this is—and cucumbers, and radishes. Isn't that pretty?" She turned to Mrs. Daily. "You make me ashamed, Mary Louise. We didn't grow a thing but weeds this year."

"And children!" Mrs. Daily said, gesturing to the roomful around her.

"And dogs," Dub added, patting Kizzy's plump belly.

"And husbands," said Daddy, walking in just then. Everybody laughed at that. There were hugs and greetings and handshakes all around. Geraldine was content. The people she loved best in the world were here now, every one.

"Any luck today, Dad?" Wing asked.

"Not bad, Sunshine. Sold yard lights to three families near the river, over where they had those burglaries last month. And another to a guy in Chappaqua—said he hated to see a man laboring for nothing on Labor Day. Nice fella." Daddy cocked his head to one side, sniffed the air. "There wouldn't happen to be some of Eleanor Brennan's world-famous chocolate chip cookies around here, would there?"

"Yes, there would," Dub said seriously. "But you can't have any till after supper or you'll be in deep trouble."

"Take it from someone who knows, right, Captain?" Wing said, laughing. Dub was short for W. W., which was short for Wallace Wayne, but Wing always called him the Captain.

Mama smiled. "There'll be home-made ice cream, too," she said, "if I can get somebody to turn the crank while I finish up in here."

"I'll do it," Mrs. Daily offered.

"No, no," Daddy said. "You're our company tonight, young lady. The boys and I can haul that contraption upstairs. We'll take turns cranking while we check on the news. How's that?"

Daddy couldn't get through an evening without Walter Cronkite. He and Wing, Dub and Sam and Kizzy retired to the TV room, while Mama and Mrs. Daily shucked the corn, and Geraldine set the table on the eating porch. Supper was always nicer out here in hot weather. It was just past sunset now. The first cooling breeze slipped through the screen and caught the checkered cloth as she shook it out, lifting it for a second like a bright parachute. A solitary bird was singing its evening song. Crickets were tuning up, calling for rain. A handful of fireflies, left over from June, flickered now and again in the shadows under the apple trees. Two bats came out to hunt, zigzagging drunkenly across the darkening sky. The last night of summer, Geraldine thought, as she placed the silverware just so, then the napkins, the vase full of wildflowers, the candles in the old brass candlesticks that always came out for special occasions.

It made her sad, a little. She hated saying goodbye, even to a season.

"Doesn't the table look pretty!" Mrs. Daily said, coming out on the porch with Mama.

"Perfect," said Mama. She gave Geraldine's shoulders a quick squeeze.

"Why is it," Geraldine asked, "that summer gets shorter every year?"

"I've often wondered," Mama said. "Time speeds

up as you get older—everyone says so. But nobody has ever been able to tell me why."

"There's an old adage," Mrs. Daily offered. " 'Lifetimes are short; only days are long.' "

Mama nodded. "That's good. Who said that?"

"I can't remember. . . ." Mrs. Daily wrinkled her brow, thinking, then laughed and shook her head. "Maybe *I* did."

"Listen!" Geraldine said suddenly. "Somebody's shooting."

"That's just the television, honey," Mama said.

Geraldine looked up. The sounds of battle floated down from the open window of the TV room, mingling with the noise of the crickets: machine gun fire, shells bursting, the dull pop! pop! of distant explosions. "Sporadic shelling in the area around Cam Lo," Walter Cronkite was saying. "Marine casualties listed at eleven dead, thirty-four wounded. . . ."

The two women looked at each other and were quiet for a minute, listening, but Geraldine tried to shut her ears. She didn't want to hear any more about the war. She knew about Vietnam, knew that halfway across the world people were shooting at each other, killing each other, but she didn't like to think about it. In a way, she didn't even believe in it, though it played on the television night after night. War was something faraway, long-ago—just pictures on the screen, like the old movies Daddy and Wing watched sometimes on the Late Show—*Flying Tigers* or *The*

Sands of Iwo Jima. Geraldine had watched some of that once. John Wayne died at the end, for heaven's sake! Who could believe a thing like that?

Mama and Mrs. Daily were worried, she knew. Wing and Sam were just shy of draft age this year. Their neighbors' boy, Eddie Zatarian, had already been drafted and was in Vietnam now. Geraldine couldn't picture that at all. Dumb old Eddie, a soldier? With his overgrown baby face and his everlasting jokes? She doubted even John Wayne could have done much with Eddie.

"Well," Mama said, collecting herself. "What was it we were talking about?"

"Time," Mrs. Daily said quietly. "How it flies."

"That it does," said Mama. And then, "Oh, my goodness—my cookies!" She turned and hurried back to the kitchen, calling over her shoulder, "Geraldine, would you please run upstairs and see how they're doing with the ice cream? Tell them we'll be ready down here in five minutes."

"Yes, ma'am."

"Oh, and honey, as long as you're going up, you might drop off those clean clothes you folded earlier."

"Yes, ma'am."

The Vietnam report was over when Geraldine stuck her head around the door. There was story about a peace march in Washington on the screen. Demonstrators were waving signs and shouting in front of the White House. Some of them were burning draft cards, getting arrested. A man wrapped in a United

States flag was lying on the grass, playing dead. Policemen were hauling him away somewhere.

"Don't those people realize they're just dragging out the war with that rot?" Daddy said. These reports always got him stirred up. He was a veteran of World War II, had served with the Marines in the Pacific—at Guadalcanal, Tarawa, Saipan. Twice he had been wounded, the second time almost fatally. "Can't they see they're hurting our own men?" His voice was louder than it had to be. The first of his war injuries had left him deaf in one ear, so he always spoke loudly, especially when he was excited.

"Mama says supper's almost ready," Geraldine broke in, hoping that would make him feel better. The whole house smiled when Daddy smiled, frowned when he frowned. "How's the ice cream coming?"

"Great," Dub answered, sticky-faced. He and Kizzy, at least, appeared undisturbed by the news. Sam and Wing had their eyes glued to the set.

"Tell your mother we'll be down in just a minute, Geraldine," Daddy said without moving. "This is nearly over—or *ought* to be," he added under his breath.

"Yes, sir," said Geraldine, closing the door quietly. She stopped in the bedrooms next, to drop off the shirts Wing wore to his part-time job at the A & P, her own shorts and socks, a pair of Dub's blue jeans, faded white at the knees, Mama's nightgown, Daddy's handkerchiefs. . . .

Geraldine closed her father's top drawer, hesitated,

then opened it again. He kept his war medals there: two little gold and purple medals, heart-shaped, tucked in between his white handkerchiefs and his black socks. She picked one up and held it for a minute in the palm of her hand. It smelled faintly of Daddy, of newspapers and chewing tobacco and Old Spice after-shave. It gave her a prickly feeling inside her stomach, even though she had held it a hundred times before.

When she was younger, the medals had frightened her. She hadn't liked to think of what they meant, of Daddy almost dying. He had tried to reassure her when she'd come to him in tears. "Now, Pumpkin," he had said, "it wasn't all bad. If it hadn't been for the war, if I hadn't met your Uncle Wallace in the Marines and gone to visit him in Texas when it was all over, well, then I'd've never met your mother, and you children would never have been born." But the medals still made her shudder.

Wing, on the other hand, had always thought they were wonderful. Sometimes, playing war with the Zatarian gang, he would even sneak them out and wear them. But that was before he and Sam had become friends.

Sam had a Purple Heart at his house, too. The army had given it to his mother after his father was killed. But Sam had never played with it, or talked about it, even. Geraldine asked about his father once. Wing had looked bullets at her to shut her up, but Sam just shook his head and said it didn't matter, it was too late, anyhow. Geraldine hadn't understood exactly what he meant by that, "too late."

She put the Purple Heart back now, closed the drawer, and ran downstairs.

2

"Geraldine, honey, hurry up! You don't want to be late your first day!"

"Yes, ma'am, I'm coming."

Geraldine was standing in front of the old-fashioned mirror over her dresser, peering hopelessly at her reflection. It was awful, just awful—she hated this stupid brassiere. She had hated it from the first moment she laid eyes on it last week, when Mama brought it home—with the groceries, for crying out loud! It came in a stupid pink box with a picture of some girl on the cover, smiling like a dope in just the bra and her underwear.

"What's *this*?" Wing had asked, grinning—he *would* have to be the first one to find it, while he was poking through the bags looking for Cheetos. "*The Littlest Angel*?"

Geraldine had gone fifty different shades of red, grabbed it away from him, flung it in the trash, and run upstairs to her room, slamming the door behind her.

"I'm not wearing that stupid thing," she said, when Mama rescued it and brought it up a few minutes later. "I *can't*."

"Now, honey," Mama said gently, "I think it's time, that's all—you're getting to be a young lady now. I imagine all your other classmates will be wearing them this year, too."

"Not the *boys*," Geraldine said bitterly, without stopping to think how dumb this sounded until it was out of her mouth.

"No," Mama agreed, smiling a little, "I guess not. But boys have problems of their own, believe me." She hugged Geraldine. "Don't worry about the bra, baby—you'll get used to it in no time."

When hell freezes over, Geraldine thought now, sighing. She could see it, for the love of Mike, through the white blouse of her uniform, and everybody else would be able to see it, too—

"Geraldine!"

"I'm coming, Mama."

Neither of her brothers was in the niftiest of moods that morning, either. Dub was nervous about starting kindergarten, and Wing, always morose on the first day of school, was having some sort of trouble with his car. Not that that was anything unusual. He had a dilapidated red Chevy he'd bought second-hand. Cost him one hundred dollars, which he really thought was some deal, until it started falling apart. Now he spent half his time putting it back together, or working more hours than he should at the supermarket so he

could pay for parts: gaskets and batteries and car-
buretors and Geraldine didn't know what all. But
Wing still loved this car, no matter how much trouble
it was. "Old Red," he called it. Personally, Geraldine
didn't see what there was to love. The noise it made,
that was the worst of it—you could hear it complain-
ing, squeaking and creaking a mile away at least. The
whole school knew when the Brennans arrived. Wing
always picked up Sam, then dropped Geraldine off at
St. Mary's on his way to the high school. And now
Dub would be coming along in the mornings, too.

"There," Wing said at last, slamming down the
hood. "That oughta do it."

"If you hold your mouths just right," Mama said
cheerfully, opening the back door for Dub. "You all
have a good day now. Dub, you're going to love kindergarten, I know it. And seventh grade, Geraldine—
just think, junior high!" She turned to Wing again,
plucked a speck of lint from his collar. "I can hardly
believe it," she said, "your senior year already. Isn't
it exciting, honey? You'll be off at college before we
know it."

Wing didn't say anything to that, just shrugged, then
went around to his door and got inside and pulled it
shut. But Geraldine saw the look on his face—the
look that meant forget college, can't you just forget
college? That look.

Mama was still calling after them as Old Red rattled
out of the driveway. "Drive carefully, Wing. Remember—precious cargo!"

"Where?" Dub asked, looking around him in the back seat.

"She means us," Geraldine explained, though she wasn't really feeling all that precious.

It helped some when they stopped at the Dailys' and Sam came out. "Hey, guys," was all he said. But the words warmed Geraldine right down to her toes, until she remembered about the bra and began to blush furiously, wondering if he'd notice.

He didn't. Or if he did, he made no sign.

Once Geraldine got to school she was glad to be wearing the bra. Mama had been right—all the other girls were wearing them, too. A few even *needed* them, for heaven's sake.

". . . a shared adventure," Sister Magdalena was saying, walking from desk to desk, looking earnestly at each student out of her round blue eyes. "That's what I would like this year to be. You're my very first class, you know, and I hope that our time together will be something really special."

Good grief—a raw recruit! thought Geraldine, trembling at her innocence. Poor Sister Magdalena— obviously, no one had warned her about Whitney Dorsey.

"Excuse me, Sister," he asked mildly during the religion review. "There's one of those commandments I never did get straight. Just what exactly *is* adultery, anyhow?"

The class, as one, drew in its breath. This was the

same question he'd asked Miss Anne Horka last year, shortly before her nervous breakdown.

Someone in the back of the room sniggered.

Sister Magdalena never blinked an eye. "Adultery is having sexual intercourse with another man's wife, or another woman's husband," she answered matter-of-factly, "or being unfaithful to your own spouse, if you are married. Is that specific enough, Mr. Dorsey?"

"Yes, Sister," Whitney mumbled meekly, sitting down again. It was the first time anyone had heard a nun say the word "sexual." Even Whitney Dorsey had been unprepared for such an event. Geraldine relaxed in her desk. It looked as if she didn't have to worry about Sister Magdalena, after all.

"See me after class," was all Sister said a week later, when she caught Geraldine reading *Gone with the Wind* instead of reviewing long division.

"Yes, Sister," Geraldine murmured. She expected to be punished, but when three o'clock came Sister gave her a stack of books, instead: *To Kill a Mockingbird* and *The Secret Garden*, *The Yearling* and *Dandelion Wine*.

"Just promise you'll finish your arithmetic first," she said, smiling, when Geraldine's eyes lit up.

"Yes, Sister," she promised. She had always been a good student, anyway, though she wasn't all that excited about fractions and past participles and molybdenum deposits in the "Mountain West." She studied because she was supposed to, because it was expected of her, because Mama and Daddy would have been so disappointed if she hadn't, the way they always were when Wing brought home a poor report card. School was what she *did*, that was all.

"Wouldn't you like to invite some of your friends over sometime, honey?" Mama asked now and then. "No, thanks," Geraldine always answered. She knew her mother worried that she wasn't more outgoing, that she didn't have lots of friends, maybe even boyfriends.

But Geraldine would rather be reading, any day, or messing around in the woods out back, down by the trout stream. These were their old stomping grounds—hers and Sam's and Wing's. She had tagged after the older boys everywhere when they were kids, doing her best not to be left out of anything. The woods were still magical to her, though she missed the guys. Sam and Wing weren't around much now, what with football practice after school—basketball was their favorite, but *any* sport would do in a pinch— and working after that. But Dub and Kizzy would walk with her lots of times. The three of them would walk and walk, crunching through the dry leaves, while the wind whipped others, freshly fallen, all around them.

"Sister says," Geraldine told Dub one bright October afternoon, "that the colors of the leaves we see in autumn are really their *true* colors—did you know that?"

"Not green?" Dub asked, surprised.

"Nope," she said. "The green is just the chlorophyll—it covers all the other colors, because it's so strong. But in the fall, when the leaves start to die, the chlorophyll goes away, and then we can see the real colors, the ones that have been hidden underneath all along."

Dub picked up a sample. "You mean when this yellow leaf was green, it was really yellow?"

Geraldine nodded. "It just *looked* green, that's all."

"But that doesn't make sense. . . ."

"Sure it does," she said. "Just think about it for a minute—" though she wasn't exactly one hundred percent certain that was what Sister had said. She'd been daydreaming in science that morning. Maybe people were a little like leaves, she thought, with hidden colors of their own. Take Sam, now—his would be golden, wouldn't it? Pure gold, like the sun. . . .

"I thought about it," said Dub.

"Well?"

"It still doesn't make any sense."

They walked past all the old places Sam had named so many years before, that first fine summer—Death Hill and Danger Hill and Darkwood Forest, the waterfall that he had called Kamikaze Leap, the rock-filled gulley that still bore its old sign, "The Valley of Stone." He was a great namer, Sam was, and for every name he would invent a story, until there were more than you could count. Only a couple of places he had left as he found them: Skunkweed Swamp was all right as it stood, he said, because what else could you call a place that smelled like that? And Three-Penny Rock was perfect. He liked the true story Wing had told about it—how when he was little he had found three shiny new pennies there, lined up in a row. Wing said, Well, it wasn't much of a story, kind of boring, really. But Sam said, No, it was one of the finest, fine and mysterious. Because the thing was, *anyone* might have left those pennies there, anyone at all—and they would never know who, and so it was a great secret.

A great secret, he had said. And Wing had been pleased. . . .

"Come down from there, Dub—you're making me nervous!" Geraldine called now to her little brother, who was sitting on a branch of the old copper beech, the one they called the Lover's Tree, nearly fifteen feet above her head. Kizzy stood among the roots, wagging her tail. Kizzy wasn't worrried; she had seen Wing and Sam climb this tree hundreds of times, using the big iron nails they had driven in the trunk as footholds years ago. It was the one place Geraldine could never follow them. She had tried, over and over, but her heart always failed her by the fourth or fifth nail. She just wasn't all that crazy about heights, was the thing. Or all that crazy, period.

"I don't want to come down—you come up today, Geraldine!"

"No, thank you."

"But it's great up here! Come on, why don't you? This is the finest tree in the world!"

"I don't have to climb it to know that, do I?"

The tree stood alone on the little piece of land Sam had named O'Malley's Island, in the middle of the stream, just below the tumbledown stone bridge. It was a very old tree, and tall—taller than any of the surrounding maples, though they grew above it on the mainland—with leaves a deep, burnished-looking color, and a smoother, lighter bark than was usual for these woods. Smoother, that is, except that it was scarred all over with hearts and dates and letters, some too old and spread apart to decipher.

"Look, Geraldine—if you come up, you can see your initials better." Dub was pointing to a particular set of letters and numbers, just beyond his reach:

GB

WB   SD

1960

Wing hadn't wanted to include her initials when the boys carved theirs, since she was too chicken to climb up. But Geraldine had started to cry—she was only six at the time—and he had said, Oh, for Pete's sake, it didn't matter. And so Sam had carved them, after all.

"I can see them just fine from here," Geraldine said. "And don't lean over like that, Dub—you'll fall!"

"No, I won't. Good grief, Geraldine—please come up here—"

"No," she said. "I can't."

Dub sighed. "Well, if you won't come up, tell me one of the stories, at least."

"I will, if you'll come down."

"Tell first. Then I'll come."

"Do you swear by the sacred tree?"

"I swear," said Dub.

"All right, then." Geraldine put out her hand and touched the gray bark lightly, lovingly. "This tree," she began, as Sam had always begun, "is no ordinary tree. This tree is a regular time machine, is what it is—three, four, maybe five hundred years old. There might be a thousand ghosts right here in this one tree, a thousand stories, all mixed up—pieces of everybody who ever lived in these woods. Indians, see there? Those diamond shapes are ancient Indian writing, secret messages from one tribe to another. And that there—that teardrop shape—that's a pioneer's mark, put there when his log cabin burned down. And over here—'Ethel and Ray, 1922'—they were secret lovers, like Romeo and Juliet, you know? Ethel was beautiful and rich, and Ray was her stable boy, and they wanted to get married. But her parents wouldn't hear of it, and so they ran away together—"

"I don't want to hear about them—tell about O'Malley," Dub commanded.

"Oh, you're just like Wing—you only like that because it's the bloodiest."

"No," said Dub. "Because it's the best."

"Maybe," Geraldine admitted. She closed her eyes, as Sam had always closed his, then stretched out her arms like a sleep-walker, as if she were trying to touch some invisible thing in the air. "I see . . . a face. A face with a beard, half grown—a young man's face. A soldier in the Continental Army, during the Revolution. I hear a name—"

"O'Malley . . . " Dub said breathlessly.

"Right," said Geraldine. "The soldier's name is O'Malley. 'Guard the bridge, O'Malley,' that's what they tell him. 'Guard it with your life. General Washington's troops must cross here tonight, at midnight.' 'Yes, sir,' says O'Malley. Just after moonrise, he hears footsteps. 'Who goes there?' he shouts. 'A friend,' comes the answer. 'Your friend and fellow patriot, Malcolm MacDougall.' 'Oh, it's you, MacDougall,' O'Malley says. 'I was afraid it was a redcoat, come to blow up the bridge.' 'Now, why would the redcoats want to blow up this old bridge?' asks MacDougall. And O'Malley—he's not too bright—he says, 'Because Washington comes tonight, of course.' 'Oh,' says MacDougall. 'What time?' 'Midnight,' says O'Malley. 'That's nice,' says MacDougall, and stabs him in the back."

"Right in the back!" Dub echoed.

"Exactly," said Geraldine. "He's a traitor, see, this MacDougall—worse than Benedict Arnold—he's been a spy for the redcoats, all along. And then he goes and gets help, and a whole bunch of British soldiers come and blow up the bridge, right over there, see? And then they sneak away, laughing." Here Geraldine laughed a fiendish laugh, just as Sam used to do, like old Snidely Whiplash on "The Bullwinkle Show"—"Nyak, nyak, nyak! And O'Malley is lying there, deader'n heck, but his ghost can't rest, he's so mad at being tricked like that. 'Guard the bridge,' he keeps saying, 'Got to guard the bridge.' And he moans and cries and makes a big storm come, thunder and lightning and wind howling and all, and the lightning strikes these big trees, three or four of them—but not the sacred Lover's Tree, of course— and they fall down across the stream just like that there—" Geraldine pointed to the log across which she had always followed Wing and Sam to the island. "So now there's a new bridge, see, and Washington can get to the other side, after all. But he never comes." Geraldine paused for effect.

"Why not?" Dub asked, knowing his cue.

"Because there's a change of plan, and he takes his troops a different way and crosses another river—the Delaware or something. And the poor old ghost, O'Malley, he's not all that smart, remember, and he never understands what's happened. So he just stays here forever and ever, guarding his bridge, waiting for General Washington. And every night at midnight, if you've got the guts to look, you can see him standing right beside this tree, where I'm standing now, with the knife still stuck in his back, moaning and crying,

'Guard the bridge—got to guard that bridge. . . .' "

Geraldine let her voice trail off.

"Don't stop," Dub pleaded. "You have to tell about the passwords, and how you've got to say 'em to prove you're a friend, if you want to come on O'Malley's Island."

"You tell me," said Geraldine. "Else how'll I know *you're* a friend?"

"Watch your back, O'Malley!" Dub shouted at the top of his lungs.

"All right, all right," said Geraldine, covering her ears. "Now come on out of that tree, friend."

Dub sighed, but an oath was an oath. "I'm coming," he said, and Geraldine watched, her heart in her mouth, as he swung himself off the branch and climbed down, limber as a monkey. Only when he touched the ground did she breathe again, and whistle to Kizzy, and turn to go. But still Dub hesitated, his fingers tracing an ancient circle in the bark.

"Geraldine?"

"What?"

"What was it Sam said happens when you carve your initials on this tree?"

"You become part of the tree, and the tree becomes part of you—you and all the others who ever put their marks here. And it's all connected some way, you know? Like something on 'The Twilight Zone'— something strange like that—" Geraldine paused, remembering how Sam's eyes had glowed when he said it, and how she had suddenly felt bigger than herself, as if a million windows were opening in her brain, and a million suns were shining through every one. "Connected," she repeated softly, "for all eternity."

"What's eternity?"

"Forever and ever and ever," said Geraldine.

"Oh," said Dub.

3

November. Brown and gray and rust-colored, all but the last leaves off the trees. A hint of snow in the air.

Football season was nearly over. Wing and Sam had already started working out with the basketball team most afternoons. Thank goodness, Geraldine thought. Wing was always easier to live with this time of year. Once the games started, his moods would swing drastically with the fortunes of the team—elated if they won, miserable if they didn't. But for now everything was hopeful, wonderful.

"I tell you what, Daily—I don't see how we can go wrong this year. I really don't. Long as Peterson hits his free throws the way he's been doing, and Kinsel can keep from breaking any more bones, and Fertitta gets that lay-up consistent—well, I mean, you and me are pretty near perfect, right? So how can we lose?"

Geraldine's favorite time of day was the twenty-minute ride to school every morning, bouncing along in the back of Old Red with Dub, while Sam and Wing held forth in front. She never said much herself.

Even with Wing in a good mood—or *especially* with him in a good mood—whatever she said, he'd have found some way to tease her. Besides, she was more and more tongue-tied around Sam these days; she didn't really know why. She was always gladder than glad to see him, but then she would be hit with a kind of clutching sensation in her chest which made it hard to breathe sometimes, much less talk. Mostly she was content just to sit with Dub in the back, listening to the older guys talking, joking around.

They argued sometimes, too, about anything and everything. One would take one side, the other, the opposite—just for contrariness it seemed to Geraldine—no matter what the issue: zone defense, the uselessness (Wing said) of advanced math, the idiocy (Sam called it) of the dress code, not to mention Vietnam.

"We don't have any business over there," Sam insisted. "It's a civil war—it doesn't have anything to do with us."

"Bull, Daily—those North Vietnamese are Communists—what're you gonna do, sit back and let 'em take over the world?"

"Bull yourself, Brennan—that's just a line the rich guys made up—the ones who manufacture weapons. They're the only ones getting anything out of this war. You don't see them sending *their* sons off to Vietnam. They draft poor jerks like Zatarian to do their dirty work. I was just reading this article—"

"You read too much, Daily, that's your whole problem. What you need to be thinking about is that hook shot of yours—most people aim for the hoop, you know, not the side of the backboard. . . ."

And then they were laughing, off on basketball again.

They were an odd pair; everyone agreed about that. "Opposites attract," Mama said, and Geraldine figured it must be true. Sam was an honor student, a natural athlete, the pride of the Class of '67. Wing was more like a walking time bomb. It was as if there were something pent up inside him, ticking away, just waiting to blow. He'd make it fine for a month or two, three months maybe, and then *Boom*! he'd explode— like the times he was almost expelled for drinking beer in the parking lot, or fighting in the locker room, or putting the Groucho Marx nose and glasses on the statue of St. Anthony in the foyer. "You're treading on thin ice, Mr. Brennan," Wing had been told over and over again, both at school, when he got caught, and at home, when he caught it. It never seemed to make much difference, as far as Geraldine could tell. If Sam's color was gold, Wing's was nearer black and blue—the color of bruises, of seventeen years' worth of butting up against life head first, fists flying.

Still, with a basketball in his hands he was a different person entirely—silver at least, like a jet plane, flying high, like his name. Maybe not the best one on the team, but really, truly good. It seemed to Geraldine that on the court Wing forgot he was small. Or else he never forgot for a minute, and his size just made him try that much harder. She couldn't have said which it was. Basketball made him happy, was all she knew.

And so November sped by as pleasantly as a chill, damp month could possibly do—better, really. Thanksgiving came and went, with the Dailys and Brennans celebrating together, as usual. The bird was perfect this year, the pumpkin pie (which Geraldine baked for the very first time) pronounced a great success.

And then it was December.

No snow yet, but the wreath was on the door, and the tree was outside in a bucket of water, and Dub was at the kitchen table, writing his eighth revised letter to S. Claus.

"How do you spell engine?"

"E-n-g-i-n-e," Mama answered. She was stirring batter for gingerbread men, while Geraldine traced angels' wings on aluminum foil. The Brennans made new decorations for the tree every year and added them to all the old ones. Their trees were getting a little ridiculous, Mama said, so loaded with homemade finery they could scarcely stand up, but that was the way the family liked them.

"I thought you already sent your letter, Captain," Wing said, stopping to eat raw dough on his way to the refrigerator. Kizzy was beside him, sniffing appreciatively.

"I did, but I forgot to say about the smoke for the

engine—it has to have smoke. That's the main part, see?"

"You know, honey," Mama began gently, "Santa Claus has such a lot of presents to deliver; he can't always give everybody just *exactly* what they ask for. He might have a hard time, fitting such a *big* train in his sack. . . ."

Dub looked at her suspiciously. Geraldine had a feeling that in his heart he knew the truth about Santa, but he was still willing to play along just in case there was something to the old story. "Well," he said finally, "do you think there's a chance?"

Geraldine could see her mother struggling. Mama loved the whole Santa Claus routine, but she wasn't one to build false hopes. "I don't think so, honey, not for that big train you saw at Sears. Not this year, anyway. But I'm sure he'll bring you something else you'll really like."

"I guess so," Dub said. Geraldine knew he was disappointed, but he was a realist, too. She could almost see his mind working, shifting gears. He crumpled his unfinished letter in a ball, tossed it into the trash can, and shrugged manfully. "It doesn't matter, anyway."

"Come on, Captain," Wing said. "Let's take Kizzy out for a run. Even old ladies have to keep in shape—right, Geriatric?" And then he winked at her and pinched her cheek. She tried to slug him, but he was too fast. He whipped past her, laughing, and next thing she knew he was out the door, and Dub and

Kizzy were running after him. And Dub was looking so cheered up that Geraldine didn't know whether to be mad or glad.

"Goodness, Geraldine—are you still here?" said Sister Magdalena, coming back into the classroom a good quarter of an hour after the final bell had rung on the following Thursday.

Geraldine looked up from *An Episode of Sparrows*, startled. She had meant to read just a couple of pages, but then she had gotten so involved that she'd lost track of the time—had forgotten where she was, even. Catford Street and its inhabitants were so clear in her mind that it was a shock to see the desks, the blackboards, and Sister Magdalena, too, standing there with her hands on her hips, shaking her head and smiling a little.

"Oh, gosh," Geraldine said, blushing, "is it late?"

"Three-fifteen, nearly," said Sister. "All the buses are gone by now."

"Oh," said Geraldine. "Shoot." She always took the bus home in the afternoon, since Wing and Sam stayed late at the high school for basketball practice.

"Well, you'd better run to the office before they close—you can call your mother to come pick you up, can't you?"

Geraldine shook her head. "Daddy has the car. But it's all right; I'll call Mama and tell her I'll walk over to St. Anthony's. Wing can take me home when he finishes practice."

Sister agreed that this sounded like a good plan. The high school was only a few blocks away. But when Geraldine arrived at the gym, Wing wasn't there. The rest of the basketball team was on the court, all right—there was Sam, looking wonderful, dribbling down the middle, then passing the ball to Philip Rawlings. But Wing was nowhere in sight.

Maybe he had to go to the bathroom, Geraldine thought. She sat down at the far end of the bleachers to wait, trying to be as inconspicuous as possible.

Five minutes passed. No Wing. Ten minutes. Geraldine had just begun to wonder if maybe he'd gone home sick or something, when Sam spotted her and waved. At the next break, he came over and sat beside her.

"Hey, fella," he said. He was breathing hard from his exercise. "What brings you here?"

"I missed my bus," she admitted, her cheeks afire. "I figured I'd ride with you and Wing when practice is over—where is Wing, anyhow?"

Sam looked puzzled. "You mean he didn't tell you?"

"Tell me what?"

Sam was silent a moment. He ran his fingers through his hair, rubbed his head as if it pained him some way. "I can't believe he didn't tell you," he said finally, then stopped again.

"Tell me *what*, Sam?" Geraldine was getting nervous now. "What is it?"

Sam took a deep breath, then let it out slowly. "He

got kicked off the team Monday. He was failing two subjects—English and math—and Sister Mary Margaret told Coach he can't play until he brings his grades up."

Geraldine's mouth fell open. "But—but he stays after school every day for practice. . . ."

Sam shook his head. "I don't know where he goes, but he's not here—hasn't been here all week. Oh, brother," he said, sighing again, "I can't believe he didn't tell you. Your parents don't know either then, I guess."

"No," said Geraldine. She would have heard if they had. She felt sick. She'd noticed Wing had been in a strange mood lately. And he and Sam were a lot quieter than usual during the ride to school the last few days. But Wing was always getting in strange moods, so Geraldine hadn't thought much about it. She had surely never thought it was anything like this, the worst possible thing that could happen to him. He must be miserable!

"They're bound to find out, anyway," Sam said. "Report cards are probably in the mail already. Ah, geez, Brennan," he murmured, more to himself than to Geraldine, "what are you trying to pull, anyway?"

Just then the coach blew the whistle for practice to resume. "Look—wait here, Geraldine," Sam said, standing up. "Phil Rawlings has a car—I'm riding with him after practice; he can take you, too."

Nobody said a word during the drive home. Sam must have explained things to Phil, because Phil seemed awfully embarrassed—he never looked Geraldine in the eye, even once. Not that she cared. She was too miserable anyway, waiting for the explosion she knew was coming.

Old Red was already in the driveway when Phil turned in. The cat must be out of the bag then, Geraldine realized, with a sinking feeling in her stomach—must have got out, surely, when Wing showed up without her. "Where's Geraldine, son?" Mama or Daddy would have said. "She was supposed to meet you at practice." And Wing would have gone red as the devil and not known what to say and finally blurted out the truth about his grades and the team—he had never been much good at lying. . . .

She looked at Sam miserably, not wanting to get out of the car. She felt guilty, for crying out loud, as if it were all *her* fault, somehow.

"Tell Wing to call me," he said, looking pretty worried himself.

She nodded and opened the door. "Thanks," she said to Phil, who mumbled some reply.

She found her family in just the state she had dreaded. Everyone was upset. Even after her parents had seen that she was safely home, she and Dub had to listen for a long time to voices raised angrily behind the kitchen door.

Her father's, first: "Why didn't you tell us right away, son? That's what really bothers me—the grades are bad enough, but being deceitful is worse—ten times worse, don't you know that?"

"I didn't want you to worry about it—it's my problem, not yours."

Now Mama's voice, anguished: "Oh, Wing, how can you say that? You're our son—don't you think we care what happens to you?"

"I didn't mean it that way, Mom. I just figured I could handle it, talk to Coach, maybe. I bet he could get Sister to change her mind. The team needs me—he knows that—I mean, I know I'm not tall or anything, but we don't have that many guys who are any good—"

"My God, boy, use your head! Do you hear what you're saying? It doesn't make any difference how much the team needs you—don't you even care about graduating?"

"Your father's right, Wing—you've just got to bring those grades up, that's the main thing. Especially with college next year. Grades are more important than any basketball team—"

"Not to me, they're not!" Wing's voice was bitter now. "I'm not smart, remember? I never was—I'm just no good at that stuff. I don't *care* what year Napoleon died, or any of it. Sam and Geraldine are the geniuses—let them go to college, if you've got to send somebody, but just get off my back, why don't you?"

"Don't speak to your mother that way, young man—you hear me?"

There was more, a lot more, but it all sounded the same, and didn't end any better—Daddy telling Wing he was grounded, Wing stomping off to his room, slamming the door, Mama crying in the kitchen. She was scared; that was the thing, what with so much talk about Vietnam and the draft and all. If Wing didn't go to college next year he'd be drafted for sure. And Wing knew it, too—Geraldine *knew* he knew it. So why didn't he have sense enough to worry, himself?

4

"Come on, Geriatric—just one more game."

"I've gotta stop now, Wing—I've got all this homework I still have to do."

"Ah, you study too hard—how much higher do you want to get than A, anyway? Come on, you gotta give me a chance to win back some of my money."

They were sitting in front of the fire on the living room rug playing gin rummy. Kizzy lay beside Wing, her chin on his knee. This game had been going on for so many years, Wing and Geraldine had grown tired of playing for points and had switched to money. The loser was supposed to pay up in the year 1975, when Geraldine turned twenty-one. So far, Wing owed her eleven thousand, four hundred seventy-six dollars. And ninety-three cents.

"But I have to finish *Robinson Crusoe* before vacation."

Wing made a face. "*Robinson Crusoe*—are you kidding? He's finished already; ten more minutes won't make any difference to him. Come on, Geriatric, my luck is changing—I can feel it."

All week Wing's mood had been black as night. He was playing with such intensity this evening that it really wasn't that much fun. She ought to just let him win, Geraldine supposed, but she had tried that once or twice before, and it only made him mad.

"It's not *luck*, Wing—face it! Can't you admit it's more than just luck?"

Wing looked at her as if she had lost her mind. "Of course not," he said. He poked the fire, sending a dazzling display of orange-red sparks dancing up the chimney. "Why would I ever admit a thing like that?"

"Because it's true."

"Shut up and deal," he said.

Geraldine dealt. She might as well, she figured; he'd drive her crazy otherwise. And anyway, even with Wing in a foul humor, there was some part of her that *wanted* to keep beating him, wanted to rub it in that she was better than he was.

"Down for three," she said, laying out her cards.

"What?" Wing cried. "You're kidding me—I was just about to gin."

"Let's see—ten, twenty, thirty-nine—that makes eleven thousand, four hundred eighty, eighty-three. Listen, don't worry—I'm sure we can work out some kind of loan when I'm twenty-one."

"Yeah, great . . ."

"It's snowing!" Dub screamed, bursting into the room. "Come look—come see—it's snowing!"

Wing and Kizzy and Geraldine jumped up. They ran with Dub to the front porch. And sure enough, snow was falling fast and thick, whirling and blowing in the wind. Already the porch steps and the rhododendron leaves were coated with white. In the yard, the last brown leaves were fast disappearing.

"I can't believe it!" Dub kept saying, bouncing around barefoot on the porch. He was supposed to have been asleep an hour ago, but Geraldine had never seen anybody so wide awake now. "Is it a blizzard? Do you think it's a blizzard, Wing?" For some reason Dub was fascinated with the idea of being buried alive in snow.

"What's going on out here?" Daddy asked, and now he and Mama were on the porch, too. "Well, look at that—I guess it's winter for sure now."

"Just in time for Christmas!" Mama exclaimed, her eyes aglow. She still got as excited as a kid, every time it snowed. "It's like a miracle, isn't it?" she said now, her voice hushed. "Oh, I hope it sticks—I hope it stays for Christmas!"

"It'll stick," Geraldine said happily. "Look—it's sticking already."

And for a moment everyone was quiet, because it really was a kind of miracle, the first snowfall of the season. For now, just for now, they had all forgotten about grades and games and basketball and bad feelings. They stood together quietly, watching, their breath turning to smoke, while the white snow fell softly, peacefully, all around the house, all around the world, as far as they could see.

"Listen," Wing said.

They listened. There was a tiny, shimmering noise in the air, as if a trillion tiny champagne glasses were being hit with a trillion tiny spoons—a magical, whispery, tinkly kind of sound.

"Must be some ice mixed in with the snow," Daddy said. "Make for bad roads tomorrow, I'm afraid."

Maybe so, thought Geraldine, maybe that's all it is, little bits of ice hitting the porch roof, and the steps, and the rhododendron leaves. But I say it's the sound of Mama's miracle.

Kizzy yawned and shivered and scratched at the door. She was too old a lady to stand here in the cold all night. The spell was broken.

"Good Lord, Dub," Mama said now, "look at you out here in your pajamas, and with no shoes, either—you'll catch double pneumonia! Come on now, it's way past your bedtime—the snow will still be here in the morning."

"Aw, Mama—"

"Aw, Captain," said Wing, tickling him. "No school tomorrow if we're lucky, right? That's the only thing that matters!"

"Right!" Dub agreed, though Geraldine didn't think he really minded kindergarten all that much. He just wanted to be exactly like Wing.

All night long the snow fell, and in the morning it was falling still. Geraldine's heart felt full to overflowing at the sight. Sam had always come over early on the first snow day, every year since they were kids. Here he was now, with a packful of something or other on his back, trudging up the white hill to the Brennans' yard like an Alpine mountain climber.

"Hey, you guys!" he shouted, waving to Geraldine and Dub, who were working on a snowman already. "Is this great, or what?"

In answer, Wing came charging out from behind the porch, pelting him with snowballs. Kizzy followed, barking happily. And then Sam was firing back, and the others joined the fray, and they were all laughing, chasing, bombarding each other.

"Tried the sleds yet?" Sam asked when the barrage had slowed down a little.

"The snow's too deep," Wing explained, pointing to a drift under the apple trees where you could just see the tip of Dub's little red toboggan. "We'll have to wait till later, when it's better packed."

"Doesn't matter," Sam said, grinning. "It's expedition time, right?"

"Right!" everybody shouted, and they all went tromping off toward the woods.

It was a perfect winter's day. The clouds were clearing now, but the sun had not yet gathered enough strength to melt the snow off the branches. Every one was lined with white; every fir tree sagged beneath its snowy burden. Now and then there was a sharp cr-aa-ck! like a rifle report when a brittle branch broke beneath its weight. The snow on the ground was so beautifully smooth that it seemed a shame to sully it with footprints, but they walked on anyway, and found that they weren't the first, after all. Again and again they came upon the tracks of animals that had crossed or gone before them on the path—deer and squirrels and a rabbit or two, tiny birds that had left delicate scritch-scratchings with their claws. Kizzy sniffed at every one and made them all laugh because she looked so important and pleased with herself and waddled so.

"Look here! Look at this!" Dub cried at each new discovery, his voice shattering the cold air as if it were so many panes of glass. "Look over here—what's this one?"

"Raccoon," Wing explained, stopping to examine the eerily human-like handprints that cut the path at an angle, then disappeared in a tangle of red-berried sticker bushes.

"Maybe not," Sam said, winking. "Might be a ghost-child came crawling through here last night, looking for somebody to play with—somebody around, say, five-and-a-half-years old—"

Dub laughed, knowing this was only one of Sam's stories, and Geraldine smiled, glad that some things never changed.

They came to the stream, where every fallen log was white coated and every rock wore a white cap, so that it looked as if a class of dunces had convened in the icy water. They stopped again to make more snowballs at Three-Penny Rock, taking turns disappearing behind snow-laden trees, shaking them just as the others appeared.

"Up the treacherous mountainside!" Sam called over his shoulder, and one by one they tackled Death Hill, laughing hysterically as they clawed and slithered their way up, Sam and Wing pulling Dub between them.

"Down the treacherous mountainside!" Wing hollered now, plunging on past Darkwood Forest to the edge of Danger Hill, where he sat himself down on the seat of his jeans and coasted to the bottom, Kizzy beside him all the way. Then he turned around, grinning, beckoning the others to follow. They did—first Sam, then Dub; then it was Geraldine's turn—

"Come on, Geriatric!" Wing shouted. "It's better than Coney Island!"

"That's what I'm afraid of," Geraldine said under her breath. Seemed as if Wing had been dragging her along on roller coasters her whole life, one way or another—up one minute, down the next. Good grief. Still, she wouldn't be left behind. Down she went, screaming half in panic, half in delight.

"Look at O'Malley's Island!" Wing shouted, running ahead again. It was a sight to see, all right. The water cascading over the broken-down arches of the old bridge had frozen into such an array of filigree and curlicues and fantastical twistings and turnings that

Geraldine gasped. It happened every year, but never in quite the same way, and every year she swore it was better than ever.

Sam whistled. "O'Malley did this," he said seriously. "He thinks if he makes his bridge look good, the general will finally come." He turned to Dub. "You ever hear the story about O'Malley, Wallace Wayne?"

"Sure," Dub answered. "Geraldine told me. Lots of times."

Sam looked pleased. "Good girl," he said. "Got to see to it that our traditions are carried on, you know." He smiled at her, and Geraldine felt finer than fine.

A redbird flew out from its perch on a snow-caked branch of the Lover's Tree and sailed overhead, chirping. Sam whistled at it. Geradine thought that if she were that bird she would fly right to Sam and light on his shoulder, and he would take her home and have her for a pet, and she would sing for him every day and sleep on his pillow at night. But this redbird flew away, missed his chance, the dummy.

"I'm hungry," Dub announced.

"Amazing," Wing said, checking his watch and chuckling. "The Captain's belly knows it's noon. What'd you do with that backpack, Daily? Got anything to eat in there?"

Sam shook his head. "Nope. Left it on your front porch, anyway. But I guess it is time to go back, isn't it? We have things to do."

Shoot, thought Geraldine. She wouldn't have minded if this morning had gone on forever.

"What kind of things?" Wing asked.

Sam grinned. "Come on!" he shouted, striking out toward the shortcut through Lone Meadow. "You'll see."

Sam had brought books in the backpack.

"You're out of your mind, Daily," said Wing, when he saw them. "We finally get a day off, and you're lugging those around?"

"Strategy," Sam said. "The team needs you back, right? And Sister says no grades, no play, right? So you—"

"Forget it, Daily—what's the use? It's another five weeks till the next report cards—the season'll be half over."

"So what?" said Sam. "Most of the conference games aren't until February—on into March if we make the play-offs again. Coach says he'll be glad to have you back, if Sister Mary Margaret says it's okay."

Wing laughed shortly. "She'll never say it's okay—are you kidding? Old M & M's had it in for me all along—she's been looking for an excuse to get me, that's all."

"That's not true, Brennan—that's just in your head. Anyway, she has to let you back, if your grades are all right after exams; a deal's a deal, right? Nuns have to keep their word—it's in their contract."

A pause. Geraldine could see Wing struggling, trying to decide whether or not to believe this. "What are you staring at, Geriatric?" he asked irritably.

"Nothing," she answered, flushing, dropping her eyes to study the knot in her bootstrings.

"So what do you say, Brennan?" Sam asked again. "It's worth a try, huh—come on, bud, give it a shot."

Another pause. Geraldine managed to keep her eyes down, but she could picture Wing, shrugging his shoulders. What his answer was she didn't know for sure. But she guessed it was okay, because in a minute the guys had disappeared into the house, taking the books with them. She let out her breath. She hadn't realized she'd been holding it.

5

Geraldine snuggled under her covers, glad of their warmth, full of special Christmas morning gladness. Then Dub was bursting into the room, shouting, "Get up, get up, it's Christmas, get up!" And now all the Brennans were standing in the hallway above the stairs, laughing and hugging and wishing each other Merry Christmas, rubbing the sleep out of their eyes—Mama and Geraldine in their flannel nightgowns, Daddy in his old blue-and-white polka-dot robe, Dub in pajamas, Wing in his traditional Christmas attire—long white underwear, red sweatshirt (now two or three sizes too small), Daddy's old Marine cap, and a mangy cotton beard that had once adorned a Wise Man in a long-gone Christmas pageant. Kizzy was decked out too, with a bright red ribbon around her neck. Catching the excitement in the air, she pounded down the stairs, her tail wagging madly, her hindquarters lumbering from side to side, then turned, looked back quizzically at the others, and pounded back up again.

Daddy knelt beside her, let her kiss his ear. "What's that, Kizzy?" he asked seriously. "What's that you say? Slim pickin's again this year?" Which was what he always said on Christmas morning.

"Go on, Daddy—go *on!*" Dub cried, dancing with impatience. Daddy had to be first down the stairs; that was the way it was always done. He grinned and descended, peeked in the living room, then looked back solemnly at the others.

"Looks like somebody's been here, all right," he said. Then he motioned for the rest of the family to follow, and they all came thundering down the stairs and crowded through the door, into the living room.

"Oh, my!" Mama exclaimed, just as if she had never seen it before, though Geraldine knew she and Daddy must have stayed up till all hours, putting on the finishing touches. And what touches! There was the loaded, glittering tree, and fragrant greenery everywhere, and the old crèche that Geraldine and Wing had made out of salt dough when they were hardly more than babies—it was pretty awful, really, with a wild-eyed camel and leering angels, but Mama loved it better than anything. On the hearth a fine fire was crackling; Geraldine never did know who it was started that fire—it was just another of the yearly Christmas mysteries. And hanging from the mantelpiece were the stockings, fat with candy. "Just one Kiss each, for good luck!" Mama said. "You don't want to ruin your breakfast!" And Geraldine laughed, because Mama always said that.

Wing turned on the radio, and Daddy sang along with Perry Como while handing out the presents, one by one:

> "*Hark! the herald angels sing*
> *Glory to the new-born King.*"

There was all the usual loot: sweaters and books (*Jane Eyre* and *Wuthering Heights*) for Geraldine, ties and fishing lures for Daddy and Wing, a dime-store necklace with matching earrings that Dub had bought for Mama—she cried as always—"And they only cost ninety-nine cents!" he told her. Kizzy gnawed contentedly on this year's rawhide bone, and Dub exclaimed about everything he opened—even the wind-up train that went round and round on a small, circular track. "Hey, neat," he said, but then he set it aside almost immediately and went back to fiddling with his new yo-yo.

"Looks like that's it," Daddy said, rustling through the sea of discarded wrappings. "Pretty good haul, I'd say."

"Great," everybody agreed.

"The best Christmas ever," Mama said. "Now, if you all will start picking up the trash in here, I'll go get breakfast started. We need to hurry if we're going to make it to eleven-thirty Mass—"

"Wait a minute," said Wing, who was kneeling behind the Christmas tree, just beneath the big bay window. "Looks like there's one more present here,

Dad." And he handed Daddy a gift the size of a shoe box.

"Well, how about that—missed one," Daddy said, peering at the tag. " 'To the Captain,' " he read.

"That's me!" Dub cried, rushing forward. "I'm the Captain!"

"This must be for you, then," said Daddy, looking quizzically at Wing. He handed the present to Dub, who sat down on the rug and started ripping at the paper. Inside there was a shoe box, all right. Dub opened it up and found another box inside that one, and then *another* box inside the second—and on and on, until there were six boxes lying open.

"This had better be good!" Daddy said, as Dub came to the last box, the tiniest one of all. But when he opened it, there was nothing inside but a little piece of paper, folded up.

"Aw, it's just a joke," Dub said, looking disappointed.

"Aren't you going to see what it says?" Wing asked.

"I guess so," Dub said, and he opened up the paper and read, " 'Dear Captain W. W. Brennan: Look in the cellar. Yours truly, S. Claus.' "

Dub looked at the others with wide eyes, and then he jumped up off the rug, tore out of the living room, through the dining room and kitchen, jerked open the cellar door, and clambered down the stairs.

"Oh, man!" Geraldine heard him shouting, before she could see what he was shouting about. "Oh, man!" And then, averting her eyes out of habit, she reached

the bottom of the stairs too, and looked where everyone else was looking—in the big room on the right,
which had always been filled with trunks and boxes
and junk of every description. But the junk had all
been cleared away now and stacked neatly against the
walls. And in its place was a train set—a wonderful
electric train set with mountains and bridges and a
whole little village, all in place on a big piece of ply-
wood balanced on a pair of saw-horses.

"Oh, man!" Dub kept saying, over and over, "oh
man oh man oh man!"

Geraldine looked at Mama with a question in her
eyes, and Mama smiled and shook her head, as if to
say, No, I didn't do it. She looked at Daddy, and he
shook *his* head, too. So she looked at Wing, who was
wearing such an unnatural expression of surprise and
innocence that she realized the truth all at once: My
gosh, she thought, it was Wing!

But Wing was saying, "How about that S. Claus? I
never knew he was such a tricky old guy!"

"I heard him," Dub said breathlessly. "I heard him
last night, up on the roof—I was sure I heard something. I didn't say anything before because I thought
it was probably just squirrels or something. But it
must've been him—I mean, look at this train! Oh,
man, I can't believe it, I just can't believe it!"

"Do you think it works?" Wing asked, still playing
dumb. "Look over here, Captain—I guess these are
the controls." Now he was plugging everything in,
showing Dub how to move the lever that operated

the engine. And then that train was flying over the tracks, and the whistle was blowing, and the smoke-stack was puffing little wisps of smoke. "Real smoke!" Dub cried. "Do you see it—do you see?"

Mama and Daddy looked at each other—sort of helplessly, Geraldine thought, as if they didn't know whether to laugh or cry. And she knew they were thinking he shouldn't have done it. Wing shouldn't have spent so much of his own money that was supposed to be for college next year. But how could they get mad, with Dub's eyes shining like stars, and Wing standing there watching him with that dopey, innocent look on his face?

They couldn't, that was all.

part two

1967

6

Geraldine wondered if it was some wise guy's idea of a joke, choosing January to be the first month of the year. To her it felt like the end of everything. Holidays over and done. Curbsides littered with the carcasses of Christmas trees. Icy roads. Breath-stopping cold. The specter of exams looming just ahead, making everybody short-tempered, jittery.

Still, there was a silver lining to that particular cloud. The one nice thing about January was that Sam was over a lot, studying with Wing. They had been plugging away steadily, the two of them, ever since that first snow day. Just about every night Geraldine could hear the steady rumbling of bass voices on the other side of the wall that separated her room from Wing's—Sam's voice, explaining and explaining, then rising, as if he were asking a question; Wing's, mumbling something, sounding unsure; Sam's, explaining again. Geraldine got so used to it she didn't care much for the nights when Sam had basketball games and couldn't come. Wing was restless then. He would jump down your throat if you looked at him crooked. Once, hours after going to bed, she was awakened by a dull thumping outside her window. She pushed the curtain aside and saw Wing out back by the light of the moon, throwing the basketball against the barn door, over and over. . . .

But most nights Sam was there, and everybody breathed easier.

"Mr. Speaker, Mr. Vice President, distinguished members of the Congress . . ."

"Come in here, everybody—the president's already started! Sam! Wing! Put the books away for a while—this concerns you! Mama! Geraldine! Dub! Hurry up, now!"

"But it's past Dub's bedtime, Arthur—"

"He can stay up late this once. Come on, now, all of you—this is important!"

Tucked away with *Wuthering Heights* in the big chair by the fireplace, lost with Catherine and her Heathcliff on the windswept moors (though she really should have been multiplying decimals), Geraldine heard the shouting and sighed. Every year Daddy made the family watch the president's State of the Union address on television. It was usually very long and boring, and Geraldine didn't understand half of it, but that didn't matter to Daddy. Reluctantly, she closed her book and climbed the steps to the TV room.

"I have come here tonight to report to you that this is a time of testing for our nation. . . ."

President Johnson's accent was so strong it sounded put on—as if it were just a big act. Sometimes comedians on television made fun of him, and then Daddy would get mad and switch the channel. He wouldn't stand for anyone mocking the president.

". . . three years ago you here in the Congress joined with me in a declaration of war on poverty. . . . I have come here to renew that pledge tonight. . . ."

"Trrrrr, trrrrrr, trrrrrr . . ."

"Dub, don't make helicopter noises while the president is talking."

"What's that burning smell?"

"Oh, for heaven's sake—my brownies for the bake sale—"

"Would everybody please *be quiet?*"

"We have now enjoyed six years of unprecedented and rewarding prosperity. . . ."

Geraldine thought about *Wuthering Heights*, how wonderfully wild and romantic it was. She loved the part about the ghost, locked outside in the storm, pleading to be let in. Her skin prickled all over again at the thought of that icy, ghostly hand holding on tightly to Mr. Lockwood's arm through the broken windowpane. It was hard to believe it was all made up more than a hundred years ago. The characters still seemed so alive—even the dead ones.

"I come now finally to Southeast Asia, and to Vietnam in particular. . . ."

"Shhh!" Daddy commanded, though nobody was talking. Geraldine felt vaguely guilty, as if her roving thoughts had shouted. She sat up straighter in her chair. Sam and Wing were leaning forward. Mama was holding on to Wing's elbow. Daddy was tilting his good ear toward the screen, so as not to miss a word. Even Dub had stopped wriggling.

"No better words could describe our present course than those once spoken by the great Thomas Jefferson: 'It is the melancholy law of human societies to be compelled sometimes to choose a great evil in order to ward off a greater evil.'

"We have chosen to fight a limited war in Vietnam, in an attempt to prevent a larger war—a war that's almost certain to follow, I believe, if the Communists succeed in overrunning and taking over South Vietnam by aggression and by force. . . .

"You will remember that we stood in Western Europe twenty years ago. Is there anyone in this chamber tonight who doubts that the course of freedom was not changed for the better because of the courage of that stand?

"Sixteen years ago we and others stopped another kind of aggression. This time it was in Korea. And imagine how different Asia might be today if we had failed to act when the Communist army of North Korea marched south. The Asia of tomorrow will be far different because we have said in Vietnam as we said sixteen years ago in Korea—'this far, and no further.' "

Nobody said anything during the applause that followed this part of the speech, but Daddy put a hand on Sam's shoulder, and Geraldine knew they were all thinking about his father. She had seen the wall full of photographs in the Dailys' living room: Captain and Mrs. Daily feeding each other cake on their wedding day; Captain Daily at the beach with a laughing baby astride his shoulders, or kissing his wife beneath a sprig of mistletoe he was holding over their heads. Framed newspaper clippings, one beginning with the headline, "Rites to be Held for Captain Harold Daily." And a medal, propped up on a table beneath the pictures in a velvet-lined case—a little heart-shaped medal, purple and gold, on a strand of purple ribbon—

"I wish I could report to you that the conflict is almost over. This I cannot do. We face more cost, more loss, and more agony. For the end is not yet.

"I cannot promise you that it will come this year or come next year. . . ."

Geraldine's stomach turned over. This wasn't a big war, was it? "Limited," that's what the president kept calling it—it wasn't nearly as big as World War II, surely, and America had won that in just four years after Pearl Harbor, hadn't it? Mama didn't need to look so pale; Wing and Sam would be all right, as long as they studied hard and went to college—college students didn't get drafted. And then it would all be over, right? What was everybody so worried about? But Daddy's face was grim, and Sam and Wing were sitting still as stones, their eyes riveted to the president's. Only Dub seemed unconcerned. He put his head in Mama's lap and went to sleep and never even heard the end of the speech.

". . . let us remember that those who expect to reap the blessings of freedom, must, like men, undergo the fatigues of supporting it. . . . Let us remember that we've been tested before, and America has never been found wanting.

" . . . we are going to persist, and we are going to succeed."

The Congress was on its feet now, applauding the president. Geraldine figured the show was over, but there was more: newscasters analyzing, congressmen commenting, a film clip of an anti-war group protesting. At this Daddy switched off the TV in disgust. "Think they can just *wish* all wars away," he said.

Geraldine looked anxiously at Sam. She was afraid he would speak up, but to her relief he didn't say anything, though she was pretty sure his cheeks were redder than they had been a minute ago.

It was Wing who spoke, as he stood and shoved his hands in his pockets. "What I don't get," he said, "is why we're holding back. Why don't we just go in there blasting and get the job done?"

Daddy shook his head. "It's not that simple, Wing. The president's got the best military minds in the world advising him—we have to trust that they know more than we do, same as we had to trust our commanding officers in the Pacific, whether we understood or not." He was quiet a moment. He must be remembering, Geraldine thought. Daddy never talked much about his war—not the bad parts, anyway. But Mama had told her that when they were first married he used to have nightmares about it sometimes, used to wake himself and her, yelling words that made no sense.

"But what if they'd been wrong, Mr. Brennan?" Sam asked quietly. "What if you'd been sure the officers were wrong—would you have followed their orders anyway?"

Daddy never hesitated. "I'd have had no choice, son; it wasn't my place to pass judgments like that. A soldier has to follow orders, or there'd be chaos—you know that."

Sam didn't reply.

"You'd go again, wouldn't you, Dad?" Wing asked now. "If you were younger, I mean, and you got called up?"

This time Daddy didn't answer right away. He looked hard at Wing and Sam both. "Yes," he said at last. "I would. And I know you boys would go too, if you were needed, if it had to be. But I hope to God it never comes to that."

"It won't," Mama said, as if she could make it so by believing firmly enough.

Geraldine didn't want to hang around talking about war. She kissed her parents good night and took *Wuthering Heights* to her room. But she couldn't quite lose herself on the moors this time, not tonight. Tonight Heathcliff had a Texas twang, and Catherine looked pale and kept talking about the enemy.

7

The next afternoon at school there was a message for Geraldine in the office, telling her she should take the bus home. Wing wouldn't be picking her up. She didn't think much about it, figured he was probably going straight to work from school, or maybe Old Red had broken down again—something like that. But when she reached home, Dub met her at the front door, wide-eyed with news.

"Wing got in a big fight at school and he beat up the other guy but Mama and Daddy had to go to the office so now he doesn't have to go back to school till next week."

"Oh, no," Geraldine groaned. "You mean he's been suspended?"

Dub nodded. "I'd be glad if I was him, wouldn't you?" But he looked worried, his eyebrows puckered like an old man's.

"Oh, no," Geraldine said again, and she hurried past him into the house, hoping to goodness he had got it all wrong.

She found her mother standing at the kitchen sink, scraping carrots. "Hello, honey," she said, just as she always did, but Geraldine could see in her face, in the sag of her shoulders, that Dub had spoken the truth.

"What happened?" she asked.

Mama sighed. "The way I understand it, Philip Rawlings made some remark about the war, some joke about the president thinking he's a cowboy, with Marines for cattle—something like that. And Wing took offense. I don't know, they said Philip was just trying to be funny, but it *did* sound pretty disrespectful—made your Daddy mad, too, when he heard. For a minute there I thought we were going to have another fight right there in the office. . . ." Mama smiled wearily; Geraldine could just picture the whole scene, how red Daddy's face would have been, hearing something like that.

"So it was really Phil who started it?" she asked hopefully.

Mama shook her head. "No. Wing admitted striking the first blow. Apparently Phil made this joke, or whatever it was, and Wing just blew up—you know what a temper he has."

Geraldine knew. "But Phil Rawlings is so *big*—what was Wing thinking about, going after a guy like that?"

"I don't know, honey. I just don't know. It must have been a pretty bad fight, though—both of them have bloody noses, black eyes coming, the works.

Sister said it took Sam and a half dozen others to pull them apart."

"Did Phil get suspended?"

Mama sighed again. "Sister let him off with a warning. That made your daddy mad, too, but Sister said the difference was that it was the first time Phil had ever been in trouble, while Wing has been warned again and again." Mama laid down the carrot she was scraping and picked up another. The sink was filling up with carrots; Geraldine wondered how on earth they would ever eat so many. "And then he didn't make things any easier for himself by glaring at Sister and saying, 'Rawlings had it coming.' " Mama lifted a hand and pushed her hair back distractedly. A piece of carrot peel stayed behind, like a limp orange ribbon. "And the worst of it is, after all of that, Sister told him she expected a letter of apology before he's to be allowed back at school. Daddy and I told him he'd have to write it, of course—he doesn't have a choice, really. But he says he won't do it—says he doesn't have anything to apologize *for*. He's up in his room right now, brooding."

Oh, brother, thought Geraldine. She remembered seeing Wing in grade school, stiff-necked, staring defiantly at a whole battery of nuns. Eddie Zatarian, two years older, had lost to him in some field day event and called him a "little cheat." Wing had seen red and made him pay. It wasn't the first time, or the last. Before Geraldine had ever started school herself, she'd had to accompany Mama on so many trips to the office that she thought of it as Wing's second home. But she couldn't recall even once hearing him say the words "I'm sorry."

"What if he *won't* apologize?" she asked now.

"He'll have to," Mama said. "That's all there is to it." She's thinking of the draft, Geraldine thought, feeling sick. Oh, Wing . . . Mama picked up another carrot. "I just don't know what gets into him, makes him blow up that way. It's as if he's mad about something all the time. What's got him so mad, do you think?"

She said it more to herself than to Geraldine, but Geraldine answered anyway, as she reached up and plucked the carrot out of her mother's hair. "I don't know, Mama," she said, wishing she could help. She felt mad herself, mad at Wing for worrying Mama so, for worrying everybody.

"Wing?" she called a few hours later, knocking timidly on the door of his room. "Supper's ready."

No answer.

"Wing—come on—it's time to eat."

Still no answer.

"Wing, are you all right? *Wing!*" She was banging on the door now.

"Cut it out," came the gruff response. "Go away."

Well, thought Geraldine, at least he's breathing. She tried again. "Mama says to come eat—"

"I'm not hungry."

"But she's been cooking all afternoon. Come on, Wing—"

"I said I'm not hungry—what are you, deaf?"

"Okay, fine. Forget it. You can starve, for all I care."

She wished it were true. She wished she didn't care.

Sam cared, too. The thought struck her just as the family—minus Wing—finished choking down their silent supper. She would call Sam, that's what she'd do. Sam would make everything okay.

Her fingers shook as she dialed the number. She knew it by heart, though she had never called before, not once in all these years.

"Hello?"

"Hello, Mrs. Daily, this is Geraldine. May I please speak to Sam?"

"Why, surely, dear—just a minute. Sam—it's Geraldine on the phone for you."

"Geraldine?"

"Hey, Sam. I need—Wing needs you," she stammered.

"I'm on my way," he answered.

He was there in five minutes. Less, actually. "How is he?" was all he said, when she opened the door for him.

"I don't know—he won't come out of his room, Sam. Everybody's tried to talk to him, but he won't listen, and he says he won't apologize, and if he doesn't he can't go back to school." She knew she was babbling. She was so relieved to see Sam that the words poured out of her in a flood. "The door's locked. He wouldn't even eat supper—there's tons left over—you want some carrot cake?"

"No, thanks. . . . I guess I'll go on up, if it's all right. We've still got a lot of studying to do."

Daddy came in from the kitchen just then, drying his hands on a dishtowel. "Glad you're here, son. Maybe you can get through to him."

Geraldine followed Sam up the stairs. She couldn't help herself.

"Brennan!" he called, knocking on the door, just as she had done earlier—but not at all timidly. "Open up—it's me."

No answer.

"Come on, Brennan—quit fooling around. We've got a lot of work ahead of us still. Exams are next week, remember?"

Nothing.

"Look, if it's this apology deal that's bothering you, we can knock that out in five minutes and then just forget it, right? We'll word it so it's okay. . . . You've made your point already—Rawlings has the broken nose to prove it."

Silence.

"Brennan, I'm not leaving here till you open this door." Sam sounded as if he were starting to lose *his* temper now. "Listen, you stay in there and all the work we've done will be for nothing—you'll just be *giving* them an excuse to keep you off the team— don't you see?" He paused. There was no reaction, so he continued. "I'll tell you what it is—you're scared—that's what. You're fixing it so you never have to take those tests—you're scared out of your mind, aren't you? Your little sister has more guts than you—you're nothing but a quitter, Brennan. You let them keep you out of school over this stupid apology and they've won, do you hear me? You've *let* them win!"

He's going too far, Geraldine thought frantically—nobody calls Wing a quitter and lives to tell about it. For a moment she heard nothing but the sound of Sam's hard breathing and her own heart pounding in her ears.

And then the door opened suddenly, violently—as if it had been kicked from the other side. And Wing was standing there, glowering. The two of them—he and Sam—stood looking at each other for a full minute. Geraldine might as well have been invisible, for all the attention they paid her. And then Wing said, "You got some mouth, you know that, Daily?" Growled it, practically.

Sam was already cool again. He shrugged. "Just doing my job, man. You think I'm gonna depend on Rawlings in a tight spot against Kirwin this year? The guy double-dribbles ice cream."

And then—Geraldine could scarcely believe her eyes—Wing smiled. Not much of a smile, but a smile, all right. Sam had done it.

"Get in here, professor," Wing muttered, and, "Get lost, Geriatric," in the same breath. But Geraldine didn't mind, not one bit.

8

Geraldine wished she could kick whatever ghoul it was who invented exams. She dreaded that queasy, gut-wrenching, palm-sweating feeling as she sat at her desk before a test was handed out. Like waiting for the guillotine, she imagined—she had read about that in *A Tale of Two Cities*—that horrible contraption the Frenchmen rigged up to chop off everybody's head in a hurry: whisht, chop, whisht, chop, whisht, chop —you next, buddy—that's what it felt like.

Still, she lived through them all, and Wing lived through his, too—his head was still attached, at least, as far as she could tell.

He'd asked for a week off from his A & P job, hadn't watched television, hadn't fooled around with Kizzy or Dub or teased her—hadn't done *anything* after handing in the letter of apology except go to school and then come home and sit in his room, study- ing. Mama and Daddy were so surprised and pleased, they seemed almost afraid to speak, afraid they'd break the spell, Geraldine supposed. Everybody crept around the house, so not the slightest noise would disturb Wing.

A couple of times Mama carried his supper upstairs on a tray. Geraldine heard her asking if there was anything she could do to help him with homework. But he always said, No thanks.

Only Sam and Kizzy were allowed in his room. Sam was there every day. He and Wing worked, while Kizzy lay at the foot of Wing's bed, snoring like a fat black bulldozer. She'd leave Wing only when Dub appeared to take her out for a run. Wing had paid him twenty-five cents a day for the service, that one week.

Geraldine would have done it for nothing. . . . But nobody asked. And now before report cards were out Mama was going crazy about Wing's eighteenth birthday, coming up on Saturday.

"We'll have a surprise party," she said, her eyes shining like a little girl's. "Eighteen's a real milestone."

"Well, sure," said Daddy. "He's earned it, hard as he's been working lately."

"But we don't even know if he passed yet," Geraldine said before she could stop herself. She didn't mean that the way it sounded—she wanted Wing to do well, sure; she'd been *praying* he would. It had just gotten to her, was all—everybody acting like the idea of Wing studying was the best thing since sliced bread. She had studied too, hadn't she? And nobody had set off any fireworks in her honor.

"Now, Pumpkin," Daddy said, and he put his arm

around Geraldine's shoulders. "You know we're proud of you, too, don't you?"

Geraldine blushed mightily, because Daddy had read her mind. It killed her, the way he did that sometimes. So she pretended it wasn't true. "Sure," she answered. "What do you think, I'm jealous or something?"

"No, of course not. . . ." Daddy looked at Mama for help.

"Your father only meant—well, maybe it seems as if we take your hard work for granted sometimes, honey. But we don't really—we're so proud, even if we forget to say it very often. It's just that Wing has always had such a difficult time in school—we'd begun to think he'd given up. But in the last month he's tried so hard. . . ."

"We just want him to know it's meant something, no matter how the grades turn out," Daddy finished.

Geraldine felt about two inches high, tops. How was it, she wondered, that anything to do with Wing always managed to make her feel eight different ways at the same time?

"That ought to keep everybody from going thirsty," Daddy said, looking at the old claw-footed bathtub filled with Cokes. "How many kids did you say are coming, Mother?"

"About twenty, I believe," Mama answered. "Sam's handling that part of it—he promised he'll have them all here by six-thirty, and then Wing should be getting home from work around seven—" She glanced at her watch. "Oh, my goodness, it's after six already and I still need to wash the lettuce and slice the pickles and tomatoes and onions—"

"I'll do it, Mama," Geraldine offered. "You go get dressed." Her mother was still wearing what she called her "working outfit": blue jeans and an old black leotard and an even older pair of ballet slippers. She and Geraldine and Dub had been hard at it all afternoon, cooking and cleaning and decorating. Geraldine still had to finish getting ready herself, but at least she had on normal clothes. She would have just died if half the senior class had seen her mother in those holey old dancing shoes.

"All right, honey, if you're sure you have time," Mama said, and then she rushed off, much to Geraldine's relief.

"I can help," Daddy offered, and while Geraldine washed the lettuce, he sliced the vegetables. The onions made him cry, so he put on a big act to make Dub laugh. "Cry me a river—boo hoo!" he sang. But the truth was he was in a great mood; they all were.

Six-twenty now, and everything looked ready. Geraldine ran up to her room, put on her Christmas sweater, and brushed her hair. Her heart was racing; Sam would be here soon, but she'd been so busy she really hadn't had time to get very nervous before this minute.

The sound of the doorbell—someone was here! Geraldine ran back downstairs and found Daddy already entertaining Sam and a couple of the guys from the team and some girls, too, including a really pretty one by the name of Maureen O'Donnell. Maureen was tall and blonde and popular and had had some dates with Sam, Geraldine knew. "Hi, Geraldine," she said. "I love that sweater!"

"Thanks," Geraldine murmured, feeling unbearably young and homely. "You look nice, too." Which was all she could think of, but didn't begin to do Maureen justice—she looked like a million dollars, was how she looked. It was discouraging. Still, Sam's smile and "Hey, fella," were better than tonic, and now the others were arriving in twos and threes, and Mama was coming downstairs with her face glowing and the awful shoes gone, and Sam and Daddy were hustling everybody into the living room: "Turn off the lights, somebody—come on, you guys, pipe down! It ought to be any minute now!"

There was a great deal of giggling and a lot of dumb jokes, and then sure enough, pretty soon there came a familiar creaking and squeaking a ways down the street. At that, Kizzy gave a glad little bark and tried to break through the crowd, but Daddy caught her by the collar and held her steady as the headlights swung into view through the window. They were Old Red's, all right—her lights always looked slightly cross-eyed.

"It's Wing! He's coming!" The word spread, and they all waited, and listened, and held their breath—

"The cars!" Geraldine cried suddenly, remembering them. "Wing will see the cars."

"Don't worry," Sam reassured her in a whisper. "We put them all the way around the bend in the road."

"Oh," said Geraldine, feeling a little silly.

Now Old Red was turning in the driveway. Geraldine could hear the motor being shut off, then the peculiar huffing and puffing, chugging and shaking that Red always put herself through afterward. The sound of the car door opening, slamming. Wing's boots crunching through the icy snow, stamping on the porch. Now the storm door was creaking open, the front door—on your mark, get set—

"*Surprise!*" everybody screamed. "*Happy Birthday!*"

"What the—" Wing stammered, and he *was* surprised; he really was—Geraldine could tell. She had seen him act, and it wasn't this convincing.

"We fooled you!" Dub yelled, pulling on Wing's belt. "We fooled you good, didn't we?"

"You sure did, Captain—you fooled me real good," Wing said. He was smiling now, laughing even. Daddy and Sam and the other guys were slapping him on the back; Mama and the girls were hugging him. Everything was wonderful, finer than fine.

Yet it struck Geraldine that there was something odd about Wing—he was smiling almost *too* broadly, and his face was too red, and his eyes looked peculiar—

Good Lord, she worried, alarmed. He hasn't been drinking, has he?

But no, surely not—Mama and Daddy didn't seem to notice anything. They were leading Wing into the dining room and dimming the lights again. Now here was the birthday cake, with eighteen candles, shining in the dark, lighting up Wing's smiling face. There wasn't "one to grow on," Geraldine had noticed earlier in the kitchen. She guessed that was Mama's way of saying Wing was all grown up now.

"Happy birthday to you, happy birthday to you, happy birthday, dear Wi-ing, happy birthday to you!" everyone sang, in about thirty different keys, Daddy's voice ringing out above all the others.

Wing took a deep breath and blew out all the candles. For a split second, the room was dark.

"Hurray!" everybody cheered, and then the lights came back on, and there was more laughter, and applause.

"Speech!" somebody yelled, and the others took up the cry. "Speech! Speech!"

Wing shook his head. "You know I'm no good at making speeches. Daily's the man for that."

Sam laughed. "No way, Brennan—your ball this time!"

Wing looked uncomfortable. "My ball, huh? Well, all right, then—I guess—I guess maybe I do have something to say. I guess now's as good a time as any."

Geraldine's stomach muscles tightened. Don't be silly, she told herself.

"First off, I'd like to say—well, I'd like to say . . . thanks," Wing stumbled, and then hesitated, as if collecting his thoughts.

Loud applause, whistles. "Great speech, Brennan," one of the guys yelled—Peterson, it was. "Is that *it?*"

Wing cleared his throat, shook his head. "One more thing," he said. He was looking at his parents now; Geraldine could see them smiling back at him. "I'd like to say—" he paused again, struggling. "I'd just like to say—this is a great party, and . . . and thanks," he finished.

More applause, laughter. "That's telling 'em, Wing!"

"Way to go, Big B!"

So that was it. The speechifying was over, and Wing was opening his presents—silly ones, mostly: a pack of chewing gum that went *bang*! when you tried to take out a stick of gum, a bottle of Wonder Bubbles, a copy of a magazine called *Towing Times*—for when Red broke down, Sam explained. Things like that. And soon everybody was eating sandwiches and cake and spilling crumbs and laughing, and John Lennon was singing "Norwegian Wood" on the record player, and some of the kids were dancing. Geraldine just hung around the edges mostly, taking snapshots with her Brownie camera, but it was a terrific party, really, couldn't have gone better.

Except that right in the middle of all the fun, when Mama and Daddy had gone upstairs to watch television, pulling Dub along with them, Maureen O'Donnell came up to Geraldine, asking if she'd seen Sam or Wing anywhere.

"They've disappeared," she said. "I haven't seen either of them for half an hour—I was afraid Wing was feeling sick, maybe. He looked sort of funny earlier."

So Geraldine wasn't the only one who thought something was wrong with Wing, after all. She craned her neck, looking around the room. "I'll find them," she said.

She went to all the regular places first—Wing's bedroom, the bathroom, the kitchen, the front porch. She walked out to Old Red, but the heap was sitting alone in the moonlit driveway, surrounded by dirty snow pockmarked with footprints. It was freezing out; Geraldine shivered and hurried back inside. She passed through the dining room, where some of the guys were standing around the demolished cake, picking at the remains of the icing. Wing and Sam weren't among them. In the kitchen again it occurred to Geraldine that maybe Wing was on the back stoop, smoking—Mama and Daddy didn't know that he smoked, but he did it all the time. On her way there she noticed that the door to the cellar was slightly ajar. Ugh. She guessed she should look down, but she hated the thought of it. Even now, with Dub's train all set up, that place gave her the creeps.

She pushed the door open the rest of the way. Somebody was down there; she could hear the sound of wheels running on the track, see the lights from the train moving, flickering in the darkness. The miniature buildings cast huge, eerie shadows on the opposite wall, but she couldn't see into the actual train room from the top of the stairs.

"Wing, is that you?"

No answer. Geraldine inched down the stairs, shuddering as she passed the snake shelves. "Wing?"

Wing and Sam were standing beside the train, staring, as the lighted engine raced along the track.

"Hey, Geriatric," Wing said, his voice flat, expressionless.

"What's with you guys? You're missing the whole party—Maureen was looking for you, Sam."

"Tell her I'm coming. I'll be up in a minute."

"All right." Geraldine turned and started back up the stairs, but something made her stop, come back down. "What's wrong, anyhow? There's something, isn't there?" She was looking at Wing.

He didn't answer, just kept on staring at the train. He stopped it, flipped a switch, started it up again, this time on a different track.

"You might as well tell her, Wing." Sam sounded mad, calling Wing by his first name; that struck Geraldine as odd. Usually, when someone called a person by his *last* name, it sounded rude, almost like an insult. But when Sam and Wing called each other Brennan and Daily, it was easy to see that they were just kidding around—that it was just another way of saying they were friends, buddies. So now when Sam said "Wing" in that cold voice, it seemed all wrong.

Wing didn't answer him.

"She might as well know now," Sam continued gruffly. "Go on, Wing—tell her."

Wing looked at Sam for a second in a way Geraldine had never seen him look at him before—as if he were disappointed, somehow. And then he shrugged, and looked back at the train. "It's no big deal," he said. "I joined the Marines, that's all."

"You *what*?" Geraldine gasped. And yet even as the words left her mouth, she realized she'd known it forever, known it all night, certainly; without ever knowing, she knew. Still, "You did *what*?" she repeated helplessly.

"I joined the Marines," he said again. "They swore me in today."

Geraldine was still struggling for air. "But—but what about school—what about college? Is this some kind of reserve deal, or what?"

"No reserves—just the regular Marines, that's all. I leave in a week. It's what I wanted."

"But—" Geraldine sputtered, "but you don't mean *now*, do you? I mean, why now? You studied so hard for exams and all—you were doing so much better—"

"You don't know anything about it, Geraldine—you don't know the first thing about it."

"So tell her," Sam said. He still sounded mad. "Tell her what you told me—tell her your big-deal reason for throwing your whole life away. Go on, tell her."

Wing shrugged again. "Tell her yourself, you know so much."

Sam looked at Geraldine. "He blew that last exam," he said. "He froze on the English lit. and just sat there for two hours, staring at the paper, getting madder and madder, thinking how now they'd never let him back on the team. And then when it was over he got up and went straight to the Marine recruiter's office—" He looked at Wing again now. "I still can't believe you did it. Even if you did fail, so what? So what if they don't let you back on the team—who cares? You don't go join the Marines because of some crummy basketball team."

"A lot you know about it," Wing growled. "How many teams you been kicked off lately?"

"But Wing," Geraldine broke in desperately, "you can't go *now*—you're not even out of high school yet—you still have to graduate."

"No, he doesn't." Sam's voice was bitter. "He's a big man now—eighteen years old—nobody can make him do anything he doesn't want to do—right, Wing?"

"That's right, Sam." Wing smiled a terrible smile, not like a real smile at all. "You got it exactly right— I always knew you were smart."

Sam didn't say anything to that. He didn't say, And I always knew you weren't. But he might as well have said it; Geraldine could practically hear the unspoken words hanging in the air between them. Fix it, Sam, she wanted to say; make everything all right, like you always do. But Sam didn't, not this time. He and Wing just stood there, glaring furiously at each other. And all the while that train was rushing around the track like a lunatic, up and down and around again—that train that ought to have been money in the bank for Wing's college, whistling away, puffing little clouds of smoke.

"Turn that thing off, why don't you? Why don't you just turn that stupid thing off?" Geraldine heard herself say.

Wing looked at her. "You want me to turn it off?"

"Yeah, that's what I said—turn it off."

"Turn the whole thing off?"

She was really upset now. "You heard me—I said turn it off, for crying out loud!"

"Okay, sure—" Wing reached over and unplugged the power pack. Immediately the cellar was plunged into blackness. Geraldine screamed.

"Not the lights, you jerk—I didn't mean the lights!" She could hear Wing laughing, feel Sam groping along the wall beside her, looking for a light switch. But he couldn't find one. He blundered instead into the shelf of Uncle Doyle's awful jars. There was a crash—and the suffocating smell of formaldehyde. And through Geraldine's mind flashed the terrible knowledge that there was a snake lying somewhere in the broken glass between Sam and her, a dead snake somewhere in the darkness at her feet.

Now Sam was grabbing her hand, pulling her up the stairs toward the sliver of light at the cracked door. "Let's get out of here," he muttered, and they left Wing alone, laughing in the dark.

Geraldine told everybody that Wing was throwing up, that he was sorry to be a party pooper and all, but he was really pretty sick. It surprised her, how she could lie to them, how she could act so calm, when there was this big cold lump in her throat. Maureen didn't seem to notice; she was really nice about it—everybody was nice. They all said thanks for the good time, and asked Geraldine to tell Wing they hoped he felt better, to please say thanks to Mr. and Mrs. Brennan—they didn't want to disturb them. "See ya," was all Sam said to her.

Geraldine sat alone in the living room, listening to the sound of the television in the room above her—Bob Hope, making jokes; the sound of the audience laughing wildly, of Mama and Papa laughing, of Wing's friends laughing at something somebody had said as they crunched through the snow on the way to their hidden cars. . . . Geraldine wondered if Wing was still laughing, down in the cellar. Part of her wanted to go and see if he was all right, but another part—the part that was in control at the moment—couldn't go down there again. She started cleaning up, instead. The place was a mess.

After a little while Mama and Daddy came downstairs. "You mean the party's over?" Mama asked, surprised. "Wasn't everybody having a good time?"

"Oh, sure, they all said to tell you they had a great time—they just had to go, is all."

"Where's Wing? Did he go with them?" Daddy asked.

"No, he's down in the cellar, playing with the train," Geraldine answered, not looking at either of her parents, looking only at the rust spot in the kitchen sink, which she was scrubbing with Ajax and steel wool as if her life depended on it. Mama and Daddy started toward the cellar door. Panic rose in Geraldine; Don't go down there, she wanted to say, Don't let him hurt you. And at the same time she almost told them the truth herself. This lump in her throat was getting so bad she thought it would burst if she didn't say anything. But what she said was, "Listen, I'm really tired— I guess I'll go to bed now."

"All right, honey." Mama squeezed her shoulders gently. "You go on. Thanks for all your help—it was a great day, wasn't it?"

"Yes, ma'am," she said. "Great." And then she kissed them both and went to bed. She hid under the covers and pulled her pillow over her head, forcing her eyelids shut, because she didn't want to be around when they found out. She didn't want to see her mother cry.

9

Geraldine couldn't sleep straight through the week, so she had to see Mama cry plenty, whether she wanted to or not.

"It's not the end of the world, Mother," Daddy told her, stroking her head while she sobbed into her folded arms on the kitchen table. "He can finish high school later—he can always go to college later." Though the truth was, Daddy looked pretty torn up about it himself.

"I just wish you had discussed it with us first, son," he told Wing. "You know I'm proud that you want to serve your country, but I'd have thought you'd come to me, talk it over, before you made such an important decision—" Daddy had some trouble with his voice then and couldn't go on.

"I'm sorry, Dad," Wing said, "but I figured you'd try to talk me out of it. You'd want me to wait. And I just couldn't wait. I had to do something—move— get out."

Get out. Get out of prison, was how it sounded to

Geraldine. And she supposed he really did feel like that, in a way. She believed he was genuinely sorry about making Mama and Daddy feel bad, but now that everybody knew, now that the decision had been made, he seemed freer, happier than Geraldine had seen him in a long time.

The only thing bothering him, she suspected, was the way Sam had been acting. He hadn't been around at all since the night of the surprise party. Geraldine knew he was busy, of course, what with basketball practice and games and everything, and she didn't see him much in the mornings anymore either, now that Wing had quit school and wasn't driving them all in Old Red. She missed those morning rides. She took the bus now, and supposed Sam's mother was dropping him at school on her way to the junior college where she taught. Once Geraldine did see him on the bus, but he was sitting way in back, and he didn't look at her. She figured he didn't want to talk.

But it was strange for Sam to stay mad at anybody, especially at Wing. Geraldine figured that maybe since they weren't used to fighting each other they didn't know how to go about making up. Or they were both too proud, or stubborn—she didn't know. One day when she couldn't stand it any longer, she asked Wing, "Hey, why don't you just go *talk* to Sam?" Wing gave her a funny look and said, "What am I supposed to do—*apologize?* What'd I do to *him*, anyway?" Geraldine started to answer; she tried to say, "Well, maybe he thinks you don't *want* to talk to him anymore," but Wing cut her off—"Just mind your own beeswax, Geriatric." And then he stalked away somewhere, and Geraldine thought, Great, just great. Here he's supposed to be a man and all, old enough to go get himself shot, and he's saying things like "Mind your own beeswax" and stomping off like a first grader.

The Thursday after Wing's birthday, Geraldine arrived home from school and found Wing waiting on the porch with Kizzy. Kizzy gave her her regular dog kiss and tail wag. She was Wing's dog, no question, but she always treated the rest of the family with great politeness. Wing watched the greeting calmly, then held out an envelope he had been hiding behind his down jacket. "Your report card came," he said, grinning and waving it at her, just out of reach.

At the sight of it, Geraldine felt that sick, awful report-card dread hit her stomach like a lump of cold oatmeal. With all the craziness over Wing, she had actually forgotten about report cards. Now that she was in junior high, her semester grades came in the mail like the high school students'. "Just give it here, Wing," she said, feeling in no mood to fool around.

"Say please," he told her, tossing the envelope from hand to hand.

"For crying out loud!" she said. Finally she managed to grab it from him in mid-air. "You didn't open it already, did you?" she asked suspiciously. She figured maybe that was why he was acting this way—he'd got some big joke rigged up inside—changed all the grades to F's or something, just to scare her.

But Wing merely laughed and shook his head. "Would I do a thing like that?"

Geraldine didn't trust him, not for a minute. Expecting the worst, she decided if he'd meddled with it she'd just open the envelope right in front of him—show him he didn't bother her one bit.

But when she unfolded the report, she found that her grades were fine—more than fine—better than she'd hoped: A's in everything but math, and she'd gotten a B in that, for which she was mightily grateful; numbers had always had a way of slipping out of her head just when she needed them. She breathed a sigh of relief.

"How'd you do?" Wing asked.

"Fine," she answered, and showed him.

"Man," he said, looking through the list. "Way to go, Geriatric." He actually sounded sincere. But then he grinned again. "Don't you want to know what *I* got?"

Geraldine wasn't sure how she was supposed to react to this, considering everything that had happened. "If you want to tell me," she said doubtfully.

Without a word, Wing pulled his crumpled report out of his shirt pocket and handed it to her.

So she looked, and then she looked again, not quite believing her eyes. Wing hadn't failed a single subject; he had C's in everything but English lit., and he had a D in that—the teacher must have decided not to make the exam count so heavily. . . .

"Wing! Is this for real?"

"It's for real, all right."

"Then you passed after all! They'll let you back on the team now, won't they? You can tell the Marines you've changed your mind—"

"But I haven't changed my mind." He was laughing now, as if it were all a big joke. "That's the funny part, see? It's too late to change my mind!"

"Too late? But it can't be—it was all a mistake, just a mistake, wasn't it, Wing? You can make them understand—"

"No, Geriatric—you don't get it. The Marines don't give a hoot about grades or teams or any of that. Once you take the oath, that's it, see? It's really pretty funny, when you think about it."

Geraldine felt sick at her stomach. "Do Mama and Daddy know?"

Wing shook his head. "Mom's taken Dub to the doctor for a check-up, and Dad's still at work. The mail just came. But listen, Geriatric, I don't want them to know—they'd get all wound up again, and it doesn't make any difference, anyway. It doesn't change anything—I figure, what the heck, I would have gone in sooner or later, anyhow."

"I think they should know, that's all—"

"No!" Wing wasn't laughing now. "They don't need to know anything about this, and don't you tell them, either—you hear me?"

"But they'll be expecting your report card when they see mine—I have to show them mine, get it signed and everything."

Wing smiled again. "I'll tell them I burned it," he said calmly. "As a matter of fact, I think I will burn it." He turned and walked into the house. Kizzy and Geraldine followed as he crossed the living room and threw the report card into the fire that was smoldering on the hearth. Geraldine knelt on the rug and watched helplessly as the white paper caught and burned with a burst of white light, then shriveled to a little black ball.

"I'll tell them I couldn't stand the sight of it, so I burned it," Wing said. "And that's no lie, either, so you don't have to look at me like that."

She guessed he was right, maybe it didn't make any difference. Nobody could stop him from joining the Marines, if that's what he wanted to do. But she wished she didn't know, all the same.

"Come on, Geriatric, do me a favor," he said seriously, almost gently. He sat beside her on the rug and put his hand on her arm. "Promise you won't tell them."

She didn't know why, exactly—maybe it was because Wing never touched her gently, never spoke to her seriously, but all of a sudden, for the first time, Geraldine believed that he was leaving—*really* leaving—that he wouldn't be around to drive her crazy anymore. So she said, "I promise," and then the next thing she knew, she was crying. She expected Wing to make fun of her, but he didn't; he just sat there quietly, while Kizzy licked her face.

"I'm sorry, Geraldine," he said after a while. "I

guess I shouldn't have told you. I'm sorry I made you feel bad."

This from Wing? And he had called her Geraldine, too. "You didn't have to tell me," she said, wondering at the strangeness of everything. "Why'd you ever tell me, anyhow?"

"I don't know," he said softly, thoughtfully, as if he were wondering, too. He picked up the poker and stirred the black ball in the fireplace. It flared up for a second, then fell into a million ashes. "I don't know," he said once more. "I guess I just wanted you to see the joke."

10

Sunday, Feb. 25, 1967

Dear Folks,

Well here I am in Parris Island South Carolina, you wouldn't beleive how hot it is right in the middle of winter, 80 degrees I heard yesterday. Pretty nice huh, I bet your jealous. Sorry I couldn't write sooner but they been keeping us pretty busy getting in shape. I thoght I was all ready in shape but that was nothing to what they want around here. You should hear our D.I.—that means Drill Instructer, Captain. His name is Sargent Price and he makes Coach Morgan look like the Easter Bunny, sort of reminds me of old M and M though. But I don't mind, the exersize is all right and I know I can make it, you did didn't you Dad.

Captain are you remembering to feed Kizzy and also take her on a lot of walks so she won't get any fatter. Maybe you shoud send her here, I guess Sargent Price could even get Kizzy in shape, ha ha.

Well I guess thats it for now, don't worry about me Mom, I am fine and the food is all right but not near as good as yours. Well so long for now, my address is on the front so you can all write back.

Yours truely,
Pvt. Arthur Wing Brennan, Jr. USMC

Wing had been in boot camp almost a month now, and Geraldine kept thinking that pretty soon they would get used to not having him around—but that hadn't happened so far. Daddy was much too loud and cheerful, telling Dub about all the different skills Wing must be learning. He made it sound like a great adventure, a game almost, but then Geraldine would watch his face during the Vietnam report on the seven o'clock news, and she could see how worried he really was. Mama tried to be cheerful, too, but even a dog food commercial could get her down. One night when the family was sitting around the television watching a boy feeding his dog Gravy Train, she left the room in such a hurry Geraldine knew she must be crying again.

Kizzy still looked everywhere for Wing. When one of the family walked in, she came bounding to the door, wagging her tail like crazy. But once she saw it wasn't Wing, her tail would droop, her dog smile disappear, and she'd pad back to the living room to lie on the rug in front of the fireplace, or up to Wing's room, where she slept each night. One afternoon Daddy went outside and started up Old Red, just to keep the battery charged, and when Kizzy heard that old engine clattering she went wild. Geraldine had to take her outside and show her it was Daddy in the driver's seat.

And now it was March. Mama's homesick month. By now, she said, the bluebonnets were beginning near the hill country, the azaleas would be blooming in her parents' garden. "I wonder," she asked, "if Wing has seen any azaleas yet. There must be azaleas in South Carolina. . . ." Then she went off to write him another letter.

Dub had stayed home from school with a bad cold, though he didn't seem to be feeling too sick at the moment. It was four in the afternoon, and Geraldine could hear him laughing at Mighty Mouse.

"Come on, Kizzy," she said, putting her head in at the door of Wing's room, where the dog was lying again at the foot of the bed. "Come on—let's go for a walk."

Kizzy lifted her head and looked at Geraldine with mild interest, thumped her tail a time or two, then dropped her chin back between her paws.

"Oh now, Kizzy, that's no good. You can't lie here moping forever—come on, girl—I said *walk*— didn't you hear me? *Walk*, Kizzy!" The word "walk" used to send the dog into a frenzy, get her so keyed up that the family would have to be careful to spell it around her. Now Geraldine had to whistle and clap and practically stand on her head to get her moving.

"We have to get some exercise, Kizzy," Geraldine explained, as the two of them passed the old barn and the apple trees and the deserted pasture and headed out along Lost Man's Way. "Mama says you're losing your girlish figure, and I hate to tell you this, but there isn't a heck of a lot to lose."

She wished it were really spring. It ought to be spring by now—that's what she always thought in March—but the woods were still cold and bare. Closed in on themselves. Waiting. Lately, Geraldine felt that she was waiting, too. But for what exactly? To turn into a swan like in the fairy tale? Or a goose, or a duck—shoot, she wasn't particular; she'd have settled for just about anything that had finished shedding its baby fat.

They walked along the usual way—past Three-Penny, Skunkweed, Darkwood, Danger. The noise of the stream was loud in Geraldine's ears, louder than usual even, as it always was this time of year with all the snow melting and the long, cold rains. Her tennis shoes were getting muddy. That was dumb, she told herself, looking at them; I should have worn my boots.

Just then Kizzy stood stock still on the path—so suddenly that Geraldine almost fell over her. "Geez, Kizzy," she complained, regaining her balance. "What's the matter?" Kizzy lifted one foot by way of reply; she strained her nose forward, pointing. Then she gave a gruff little bark, deep in her throat. "Woof," she said—Kizzy was the only dog Geraldine knew who actually said "woof"—and took off running, barreling down Death Hill like a two-ton cannonball.

"Good grief, what is it, Kizzy?" Geraldine shaded her eyes and looked. There was someone walking down by the stream. "Leave him alone, Kizzy—come back, girl!" she shouted. Kizzy would never hurt a fly, but sometimes she barked at strangers and frightened them. She considered all the land back here Brennan territory, no matter what the county books had to say about it.

But this time she wasn't barking, and as Geraldine scrambled after her, she saw why not. It wasn't a stranger at all—it was Sam. Geraldine was skating down the muddy hillside so fast by now that she almost crashed right into him, almost knocked all three of them right into the stream.

"Whoa—hey, fella," he said, catching her, smiling his golden smile.

Geraldine blushed. "Hey, Sam," she said. "Sorry—I didn't mean to run you over—I thought Kizzy was going after some stranger—"

"It's okay, it's okay," he said, laughing. "I'm glad to see you, both of you. Hey, Kizzy—hey, old girl!"

Kizzy was nosing all around him, wagging her tail like mad, sniffing at his clothes.

"She's looking for Wing again," Geraldine explained. "She doesn't understand about the Marines."

"Oh," Sam said, and he squatted down next to Kizzy, and let her kiss him, and scratched her behind the ears, the way she liked Wing to do. "Poor old girl, what'sa matter—lost your buddy, huh?"

Geraldine sat down on a rock beside them, blessing Kizzy for finding Sam, wishing she were older and looked like Maureen O'Donnell. For a minute, neither spoke. Then, "How's Wing doing, anyway?" Sam asked softly, almost shyly, as if he were embarrassed. He wasn't looking at her, just concentrating, it appeared, on Kizzy's collar.

"Fine—he's doing just fine," Geraldine answered. "He says they're working everybody pretty hard, and some of the guys are having a bad time trying to make the grade, but he says he's all right."

Sam nodded. "I figured he'd be fine—I figured he wouldn't have any trouble. They don't come any tougher than Brennan."

"I guess not," Geraldine said, glad that Sam wasn't sounding mad at Wing anymore.

"Has he heard if—" he began now, and then stopped. "Does he know where he's going yet?"

Geraldine shook her head. "Not yet—not for absolute certain. But he's pretty sure he'll be going on somewhere for further training after boot camp— maybe Quantico, in Virginia. Then he ought to get a leave when that's over, so he'll come home for a while, probably thirty days. And after that I guess it'll be Vietnam."

Sam was quiet again. "That doesn't leave much time," he said finally.

"Time for what?"

He looked at Geraldine now, as if he were trying to decide something. Then he shook his head. "Nothing," he said. "I'm just thinking out loud." He stood up. "Where are you guys headed?"

"Nowhere, really. Just walking."

"Mind if I walk along?"

"Sure—I mean, no—I mean, that'd be fine," Geraldine blundered, and Sam grinned, and put out his hand to help her up. She took it, scarcely believing her good fortune, and the three of them continued along the path, crossing the log bridge at O'Malley's Island, and coming at last to the Lover's Tree.

What a fine old tree it was. Right now it was bare, but in a month or so it would be the loveliest thing in the world, covered with little red blossoms, and bright red leaves just beginning—the queen of the forest, all in red, alone among the delicate new spring green of the maples. Later in the year its leaves would darken to a deep copper color. That time was beautiful, too, but the week of the blossoming was best. Last year Geraldine had miscalculated and missed it altogether. She wouldn't miss it this spring; she hoped she'd never miss it again.

"Look up there," Sam said. "You can still see our old initials."

Geraldine nodded, remembering the day he had carved them—so long ago, and yet like yesterday, too, as if time really did stop at the tree, the way he used to say it did.

"Do you remember the oath?" he asked now.

"Sure," she said, grinning. "I taught it to Dub, too." She touched the gray bark and closed her eyes. "I swear by the sacred Lover's Tree, eternal friendship and everlasting loyalty. All for one and one for all." She opened her eyes. "I guess we stole some of that from *The Three Musketeers*, didn't we?"

"I guess so," Sam said, and he looked at her curiously. "You really do remember. . . . I mean, that's amazing—you were such a little kid back then."

Does that mean he's noticed I've grown up? Geraldine wondered. Her cheeks felt hot again. She shrugged. "Sure, I remember," she said. "I remember all of it. Those were some great times."

"They were, weren't they?" Sam agreed. Kizzy put her head in his hand, wanting to be petted. He chuckled and obliged. "Listen, Geraldine," he said, after a while, "will you do me a favor?"

"Sure."

"Just keep on remembering, that's all," he said, and he touched her hair lightly, brushing off a bit of twig that had caught in it. It was almost a caress, that touch; it left Geraldine weak, shaking.

"Sure," she said again. As if she could ever forget, even if she wanted to.

11

By mid-April, Dub's feet wouldn't fit in his shoes any-more.

"I declare, I believe you've gotten bigger over-night," Mama sighed. "Another growth spurt, I guess."

Dub looked shocked. "I am not either!" he cried.

"You are not either *what*, honey?"

"A gross squirt."

"Oh, Dub," Mama said, laughing and hugging him, "that's not what I said. . . ."

An hour later the family was driving over to the Willow Crossing Shopping Center in the heart of town. Geraldine's shoes were getting pretty tight themselves, Mama needed a new teakettle—she had burned up the last one—and Daddy wanted to take a look at the fishing lures Bob's Sport and Tackle Shop had on sale.

> *"I had a dream, dear; you had one, too,*
> *Mine was the sweetest; it was of you. . . ."*

Daddy sang, making Mama smile, as the station wagon turned into the crowded parking lot—it looked as if everybody in town had had the same idea about shopping that Saturday morning. The weather was fine, just a little on the chilly side, white clouds grazing in the blue sky, crocuses and daffodils pushing up here and there in the small garden plots outside the stores.

"All right, now," Daddy said, as they all climbed out of the car. "We need a plan. Let's say we do the shoes first—how's that?"

Geraldine groaned inwardly. She had hoped the sale at the sporting goods store would keep him occupied. Daddy was crazy about sales—always got so excited about bargains that there was no refusing him when he found what he thought was a great buy. Geraldine had spent all last summer in turquoise tennis shoes from Shoe City, because she hadn't known how to say no when he walked up to her holding them, his eyes shining with that "only-three-fifty— can-you-believe-it?" look. They had lasted forever, too, those awful shoes, because Daddy always insisted on buying everything at least two sizes too big. Poor Wing never *had* grown into that last pair of boots. . . .

"The shoe store first," Daddy was saying now, "and then you can go with Mama to Walgreen's—"

"Look!" Dub interrupted. "That's Sam over there! Hey, Sam!"

Geraldine's heart gave a glad little leap. It was Sam, all right, standing just across the parking lot from them, in front of the five and dime. He had a stackful of flyers he was giving out to shoppers as they passed by.

"Hey, Sam!" Dub hollered again. This time Sam heard him. He looked up, saw who it was, and then—it seemed to take him longer than it should have—he raised a hand in greeting.

"I'll bet he's selling raffle tickets to raise money for the baseball team," Mama said. "You remember, he and Wing did that last year. We really ought to buy at least one, don't you think?"

"Well, sure," Daddy said.

Dub had already run ahead and was talking to Sam when Geraldine and her parents caught up.

"Hello there, Sam!" Daddy boomed, smiling and shaking hands. "We've come to buy you out, make you a rich man. My bride here has her heart set on winning the crown jewels—got any on hand?"

"No, sir." Sam looked red in the face, uncomfortable. "No, sir, no jewels today."

"Oh, well, that's all right," Mama said. "I guess I'll settle for a chocolate cake. You all doing cakes again this year, honey?"

"No, ma'am, no cakes, either."

"Well, don't keep us in suspense, Sam," Daddy said. "Now, what've you got for prizes?"

By now a half dozen people had stopped to hear the answer. With Daddy talking so loudly, it must have sounded a little like some sort of show.

Sam hesitated. Then, wordlessly, he handed Daddy one of the flyers.

Daddy took it, began to read. As his eyes traveled down the page, his face changed. His smile lingered at first in a disembodied way, as if it weren't really connected to him—like the Cheshire Cat's, it struck Geraldine—and then faded altogether. The color began to rise in Daddy's cheeks, too, as it had in Sam's. Both their faces were red as apples.

"What is it? What's the matter?" Dub asked, but no one spoke. A couple of bystanders grew bored, moved on, but others stayed, held by the curious tension in the air.

Geraldine couldn't take it any longer. Mama had always taught her it was impolite to read over somebody's shoulder, but she and Geraldine both leaned in now, trying to see what was on the paper.

HELP BRING ABOUT PEACE IN SOUTH-EAST ASIA, it began. WHAT YOU CAN DO TO HELP:

1. READ!! The United States is currently involved in an immoral war, in which thousands of innocent men, women, and children are being needlessly slaughtered, day after day. We are not getting the full story. The American news coverage has been largely limited to press releases handed out by the government, which has a vested interest in keeping the conflict

alive. War is good for business, the theory goes. <u>But it is a deadly business that has at its heart the taking of human life</u>.

Attached you will find copies of articles by leading newspapermen, not only from America, but from countries all over the world. Included are interviews with veterans who have witnessed these atrocities firsthand. READ THEM!! LEARN THE TRUTH!!

2. <u>WRITE!!</u> If you believe that the War in Vietnam is wrong, write your congressman today; tell him you <u>do not support</u> the administration's present policy.

3. <u>SPEAK OUT!!</u> As Americans, this is our right, our duty. Silence makes us all accomplices to murder. Every day we delay more lives are wasted. <u>THIS WAR MUST BE STOPPED AT ALL COSTS!!</u>

Geraldine's eyes flew over the words, so quickly that she didn't fully comprehend their meaning. She would have read them a second time, but she never had the chance, because suddenly Daddy crushed the flyer in his fist and tossed it in the gutter. "Trash," he muttered. "Who writes this trash, anyway?" His voice was lower than usual, much lower, but Geraldine had never heard him sound so angry. She felt sick, frightened. Daddy was still looking at Sam. "Where'd you get this trash, Sam? Don't you know what it says?"

"Yes, sir," Sam said. Perspiration was gathering on

his forehead, shining, though the air was cool. "Yes, sir, I know what it says. I wrote it."

For an instant Geraldine thought wildly that Daddy was going to hit him. Run, Sam! she almost cried out. But Daddy made no move, though his eyes were blazing, dangerous. "And you *believe* it?" he asked now, his tone incredulous.

Sam stood his ground. "Yes, sir," he said. "I do."

There was another awful pause. Vaguely, Geraldine noticed that her arm was throbbing. Her mother was holding it in a vise-like grip.

"Well then," Daddy said at last, in that low, terrible voice, "I guess we don't have anything left to say to each other."

It wasn't until the family was in the car, all silent, that Geraldine remembered they hadn't bought a single thing, not shoes, or lures, or teakettles.

All that afternoon Geraldine wandered miserably through the woods, trying to think, trying to sort out what had happened.

Was Sam a traitor?

Daddy seemed to think so. He had always said that the protesters were no better than the traitors, that they were really just prolonging the war with their yammering about peace. That was what General Westmoreland had said in the paper the other day. He claimed the anti-war people were aiding and abetting the enemy, encouraging them to keep fighting by making it look as if Americans didn't support their own soldiers.

But Sam was no traitor, was he? Not *Sam*—Geraldine couldn't believe it. So what was he thinking of, anyway? She knew he was mad at Wing for dropping out of school and joining the Marines, she knew he had never thought the war was such a hot idea, but this was going too far, wasn't it? That paper he was handing out was so concerned about all those innocent women and children getting killed; okay, Sam was sorry for those people—Geraldine was sorry for them, too, and she bet Wing was sorry for them, and the other soldiers were sorry, and the generals, and even the president—they were all trying to help those people, weren't they? Sam wasn't the only one. *Somebody* over there must not want the Communists to take over. The United States didn't just make it all up— Americans didn't start this stupid war, did they? And anyway, where did Sam come off caring more for those people than he did for his own friend? He didn't even *know* those people—Wing was the one he knew, the one he ought to care about.

Sam, a traitor?

"I don't believe it's as bad as it looked," Mama said finally; it was midway through supper before they could bring themselves to talk about it. "Surely Sam *means* well—just because he's against the war doesn't mean he's against Wing."

Geraldine looked up hopefully, even though Mama always took up for everybody, even criminals. But

Daddy said, "It all amounts to the same thing, Mother. Didn't you read what he's saying in that fool paper? Calling Americans murderers—that's what he's doing. The Communists couldn't have written better propaganda themselves!"

"Maybe if you talked to him," Geraldine began, "maybe you could explain it to him, get him to stop saying those things."

"If he doesn't know where I stand by now, he never will," Daddy said. "How could he *not* know? Sam's a smart boy, there's no question about that. Maybe a little too smart. If he wants to talk sense, he knows where to find me." Daddy pushed back from the table, then rose slowly, wearily, as if all his bones pained him. "I wouldn't have thought it of him," he said, "not in a million years."

The following Monday at noon, Geraldine sat down in the cafeteria at school, took out her lunch, and burst into tears.

Sister Magdalena was at her side almost immediately. "What's the matter, Geraldine?" she asked.

Geraldine shook her head hopelessly. Sobs convulsed her whole body, rose from her chest in racking waves. "I hate—I hate—baloney!" was all she could manage to choke out.

"Is there anything else?" Sister asked gently. But Geraldine only shook her head again and gritted her teeth until the spasms finally subsided a little. She really *did* hate baloney. And there *wasn't* anything else, exactly; there was *everything* else—too much to say, too much to explain.

That night she discovered she had started her first period. It made her feel miserable, mostly, and scared a little, and embarrassed a lot. Mama helped her get cleaned up and comfortable, hugged her, told her how exciting, how wonderful it was, entering this new time in life.

"I'm so proud of you, honey," she said. Which puzzled Geraldine; it wasn't as if she had done anything on purpose, for heaven's sake.

The strangest thing about it was what crossed her mind briefly—just for a second—when she was going to bed that night. I wish I could tell Sam, she thought. And then she was shocked at herself for thinking such an awful thing—such a sick thing, really. Is this what's meant by an impure thought? she wondered.

But it didn't feel impure; it felt lonely.

Was Sam a traitor?

Wondering, she cried herself to sleep.

12

So far Daddy had been sure three different planes were Wing's, even though his flight wasn't due into LaGuardia Airport for another ten minutes. Geraldine watched Mama jump around like a jack-in-the-box, rushing over to the window to look out, sitting down, getting a drink of water at the fountain, sitting down again, then starting back to the window for another look. Geraldine sighed. She was nervous enough herself, though she didn't know why. It was just Wing coming home on leave, right? He hadn't turned into John Wayne, for heaven's sake.

Still—it had been such a long time since they'd seen him. More than three months. And so much had happened. It was June now—a whole season of the year had come and gone. Two-and-a-half lifetimes to a mosquito, Geraldine figured; she had studied insects in science spring semester. The small brown bird that had worked so patiently all during April, building a nest on the front porch, had already laid her eggs, sat on them, hatched them, and taught her babies to fly;

the nest was deserted now. Dub had lost three teeth, Daddy had watched one hundred sixteen newscasts, Mama had cooked three hundred forty-eight meals. Geraldine had grown an inch, read eleven books, stubbed her toe twice, learned all the tributaries of the Mississippi River. Become a woman, for crying out loud—that was what Mary Edna Stallworth's mother called it.

And Sam—well.

Geraldine wondered what Wing would think if he knew about Sam and this peace business. They'd pretty much agreed not to mention any of it to him in their letters. But Geraldine was afraid that sooner or later he was bound to hear it from somebody. The whole town knew by now. Just a couple of weeks ago, Sam had been out in front of the A & P, trying to get signatures on some petition, and Mr. Zatarian, what with Eddie in the army and all, had gotten really steamed and called the police—said Sam was creating a public nuisance. Sam might have been arrested in a big city, but it turned out that the policeman they sent had gone to St. Anthony's and was a big basketball fan. So when he saw that it was one of the stars of the team who was causing the disturbance, he let Sam go with a warning. Geraldine couldn't believe her ears when she heard—*Sam*, nearly getting put in jail? The whole thing was too stupid for words, made her want to throw up.

Sam had graduated with honors last week. The Brennans had received an invitation in the mail from his mother, but they didn't go—couldn't go, really, after all that had happened. Though Mama did call Mrs. Daily to extend her regrets. Geraldine heard her talking on the phone and had to look to see that it really *was* Mama—she had sounded stiff, strange—not like her usual self at all.

"Mary Louise?" she had said. "It's Eleanor. . . . Well, I know, it's just been too long, hasn't it, but you know how hectic things always get this time of year. . . . Well, no, as a matter of fact, that's why I'm calling; I'm afraid we won't be able to make it. It was so sweet of you and Sam to invite us, but Arthur hasn't been feeling too well. . . . No, no, nothing serious; he's just a little under the weather, is all. . . ."

This wasn't a lie, exactly; Daddy really hadn't been feeling too well.

"But please tell Sam congratulations for us. . . . Oh, yes, Wing was one of the top ten percent in his platoon during boot camp—they tell me that's quite an accomplishment. . . . Has Sam made his plans for next year? . . . That's marvelous, Mary Louise. You must be so proud. . . ."

"What's marvelous?" Geraldine asked, when Mama had hung up.

"Sam has been awarded a scholarship to Georgetown University, in Washington D.C.," Mama explained. "His mother is just thrilled. I'm glad for her."

But Geraldine knew it was hard for Mama to hear that, when she and Daddy had always had their hearts set on Wing going to college. And so she heard herself saying, "Maybe Sam can get himself arrested for real in Washington, huh? Maybe he'll get arrested with all those big-time protesters and get his scholarship taken away, and then he'll get drafted and end up having to go to Vietnam after all, just like Wing; maybe then he'll be sorry for saying all those things—"

"You don't mean that, honey," Mama said quietly.

"Yes, I do," Geraldine insisted. But she didn't, not exactly. She just wanted everything to get back to normal. Why couldn't this be a normal war like World War II, where everybody cheered for the soldiers and America won and then it was over. . . .

"Here it is—this is the one!" Daddy was shouting now, and sure enough, it looked as if he was really right this time. The plane was coming in, its lights bright in the dark sky, its engines filling the air with their roaring. And now it was down, taxiing along the runway; signalmen were rushing to meet it, waving their arms—ants giving orders to an eagle. Now the portable steps were rolled out, the plane door opened. The stewardess was helping two old ladies in hats, a short man with glasses, a young woman with a baby—

And Wing.

"There he is! There he is!" Dub shrieked, and now Geraldine could see him, too. The uniform had taken her by surprise at first, but then she recognized him, just as he caught sight of the family. He smiled and waved; he was hurrying down the steps now, across the tarmac, through the door.

And at last everyone was hugging him together and

laughing and talking at the same time—Mama was crying again, and Daddy was pounding him on the back and saying, "Well, well, Sunshine—looking pretty sharp there, Marine!" and Dub was talking a mile a minute, asking a million questions. Geraldine hung back a little, feeling suddenly shy. It was just Wing, she knew, but he looked different, somehow, like a different person, almost—taller even, so straight-backed and handsome in that uniform.

"Hey, Geriatric," he said, smiling at her. "Have a piece of gum." So she took it, like a dummy, and it went *bang!* naturally, and she jumped, and he laughed like crazy. "Didjya miss me?" he asked, giving her shoulders a quick squeeze.

"Heck, no," she told him.

"Guess I'll run over to Daily's this afternoon, see if he wants to do a little fishing," Wing said at lunch the next day—breakfast for him, really, since he had slept most of the morning. Geraldine and Mama looked at each other, not saying anything, not knowing what to say. Daddy picked up a piece of bread, began to butter it carefully. He had come home for lunch especially to visit with Wing on his first day with the family, but now he was resorting to his deafness and pretending not to have heard—Geraldine was sure that was what he was doing.

"Can I go, too?" Dub asked.

"Sure thing, Captain," Wing said. "You dig us some good worms while I see what Daily's up to—shouldn't take me more than a half hour. Then we'll come back by here and get you. How's that?"

"Great," Dub said happily, running for his bucket and spade.

"How about you, Geriatric?" Wing asked. "You want to come?"

Fishing with the guys had always been a special treat for Geraldine. The Brennans had a four-person rowboat. When Daddy and Sam and Wing were all going out on the reservoir, she and Dub had to take turns for the extra place. But Daddy would be going back to work today. "Well—well, sure," she stammered, too surprised to think it through. She had imagined Wing wouldn't care to see Sam at all, since they had parted mad the night of the birthday party. (Lord, but it seemed like a million years ago now!) She'd forgotten that wasn't Wing's way after a quarrel—*she* of all people should have remembered—that though he'd never apologize or anything close, after a while he'd just pick up as if nothing had happened.

When he was finished eating, Wing said so long to his father, hugged his mother—for a second, Geraldine thought Mama might not let him go, she was holding on so tightly—and then he strode out the front door, whistling. Kizzy trotted along at his side; she hadn't left it since his return.

"Will Sam tell him, do you think?" Mama asked fearfully, watching out the window as Wing tried to crank up Old Red.

"I have no idea," Daddy said. He shook his head.

It occurred to Geraldine that it was grayer than it had been just a few months ago, before Wing left for boot camp. "I used to think I knew that boy, knew how his mind worked. I'd have bet my bottom dollar on Sam Daily." Daddy took off his reading glasses, rubbed his eyes. "But I was wrong, wasn't I?"

Don't tell him, Sam, Geraldine prayed. Just be his friend again, like always—just forget this other junk and be his friend, so everything can be the way it was. Please, Sam . . .

Wing didn't come back in half an hour, or an hour. He didn't come back all afternoon, or for supper. Mama was frantic. She called Sam's house and spoke to Mrs. Daily, but didn't learn anything—Mrs. Daily had been out all day, she said, and the house was empty when she returned. She didn't know where Sam was, either.

Dub waited patiently with his worms until almost dark, and was still waiting at ten o'clock, when he finally fell asleep on the living room couch. Geraldine waited, too. She took *How Green Was My Valley* to bed with her at eleven and tried to read, but her mind kept wandering, waiting for Wing, listening for the sound of his return.

She heard it, finally, just before three in the morning. Heard Old Red on the road, turning in at the driveway. Heard Mama and Daddy going downstairs, waiting for Wing on the porch. Heard the jingle of Kizzy's dog tags, the sound of Wing's voice, saying something—she couldn't tell what—and Daddy's voice, then Mama's, answering. Heard their footsteps, coming back upstairs. As they passed her door, Geraldine got up, looked out—she couldn't help it—she had to see if Wing was all right.

She smelled him even before she saw him—the sour smell of too much liquor; she had smelled it on his breath once or twice, and she knew right away what it was. He was drunk, really drunk. She could see it in everything about him, in the way he stumbled, and leaned so heavily on Daddy's arm. She knew it, though she had seen drunks only on television or in the movies. But this was worse, much worse—not funny like Willie Lump Lump.

"Go back to bed, Geraldine," Mama said when she saw her.

Geraldine couldn't move. Wing was looking at her now, and she saw his eyes, how swollen they were, and the cut on his lip. He'd been fighting again, then. And Geraldine felt it in the pit of her stomach: he had been fighting with Sam. Wing looked at her with hurtful, hurting eyes and a crooked smile. "Watch your back, O'Malley," he said to her—or maybe it wasn't really *to* her—just *at* her. "You better watch your back, you hear me? Old MacDougall's at it again."

Nobody in the house mentioned Sam Daily for the rest of Wing's leave. There were no more drunken homecomings, no more fights, no more unpleasant scenes of any kind. Dub got to fish all he wanted, and Geraldine too. There was plenty of room for Daddy to take all three of his children in the rowboat, without Sam along.

13

July 20, 1967

Dear Folks,

Well here I am over the Pacific Ocean, how about that Captain. We left Okinawa an hour ago, not much to see so far but clouds out my window. Listen I just wanted to thank all you guys for everything, I mean while I was home. It was really great especially Mom's fried chicken, and hey Dad thanks for the St. Christopher Medal. Its really something how it saw you through W. W. II and all, I'll take good care of it, I promise you that. Well I guess that's it for now, there's this guy next to me whose asleep, snoring so loud you wouldn't beleive it, he sounds like one of those what do you call them, jackhammers. I guess I should sleep too, we still got a ways to go. But this guy is really snoring and anyway I don't want to miss the landing, that should be intresting.

Love,
Wing

July 25, 1967

Dear Folks,

Well here I am in-country, that's how they say it around here Captain. Happy birthday Dad, I know that's today and I'm sorry this will get to you late but this is the first chance I had to write. This place is sure different, I can tell you that all ready, not much to look at and hot like you wouldn't beleive. Boy and it sure can rain, I never saw rain like this, no space between the drops, more like standing under the waterfall at home. One thing around here, all of a sudden I am tall, these Vietnamese are hardly even five feet but the guys say don't let that fool you they are plenty tough. And you should hear them talk, its really like being in a forein country all right.

So far I'm still in Da Nang where we landed, so far this war hasn't been much, a coupel patrols but nothing happened, nothing to worry about Mom, the guys say just use your head and you'll be all right. I am getting in some practice on gin rummy with a guy named Hopkins from Kentucky, he was the one next to me on the plane that snored so loud, turns out he's a pretty funny guy. He showed me a trick or two with the cards, I guess I can beat you now Geriatrick so watch out.

Well I guess that's about it, you guys can write

me to the address on the envelope and it will get to me wherever I end up. Tell Kizzy I said woof and go easy on the dog food.

Love,
Private First Class
A. Wing Brennan, Jr., USMC

Dear Wing,

How are you, fine I hop. We got your letter, that was funny abowt the guy who thot he was being attaked at nite and then in the morning it was only a bannana tree. Kizzy is ok but still fat, well by.

Love,
Dub or the captin

September 20, 1967

Dear Wing,

We really enjoyed your letter. Dub laughed and laughed about Hopkins shooting the banana tree, and then he sat right down and wrote you back—pretty good for a first grader, don't you think? I'm putting his letter in with mine.

Are you sure you're okay? You never say anything bad in your letters but Mama thinks maybe you leave out the bad parts on purpose. You wouldn't do that, would you? You know Mama, she thinks she has to worry all the time to keep bad things from happening.

Everything is okay around here, pretty normal, I guess. School is the same as always, except this year I have Mrs. Fogarty. She isn't nearly as smart or as nice as Sister Magdalena, but I guess that's the way it goes. You wouldn't believe what she told us about fat cells the other day. She said when you lose weight, your fat cells don't get destroyed, they just shrink up. And then the first time you take a little bite of ice cream or something—Zap! They swell up all over again, and you're as fat as ever. I think that's what she said, anyhow. I had no idea eighth grade would be so depressing. I don't know, though, maybe it'll come in handy someday. Maybe I'll write a great tragedy, like "Hamlet," and call it "Old Fat Cells Never Die."

The Bulldogs aren't doing very well this year without you.and They're looking pretty sad, to tell you the truth. They already lost their first two games.

I almost forgot, Sister Magdalena said to tell you she's saying an extra rosary for you every week. I guess that ought to keep you covered, that plus Mama and Daddy going to six o'clock Mass every morning. I'd go, too, but they asked me to stay around here with Dub and make sure he gets up in time for school. You know what a hard time he has waking up on school days, sort of reminds me of somebody else I know.

It's getting pretty late so I'd better wind this up

for now. Just one more thing—tell your friend
Hopkins he's just wasting his time trying to teach
you gin rummy tricks, I know them all already.
Well, so long for now. Take care of yourself.

Love,
Geraldine

P. S. Dub is getting new teeth in front. They are
the biggest teeth you ever saw, but he's pretty excited about them anyway.

Friday, October 13, 1967

Dear Folks,

Hey Dad how bout them Cards anyhow? The
world series games didn't come on the radio over
here til five in the morning but Hopkins and me
and some of the others got up early to listen. We
missed some parts because of incoming, it was just
a coupel shells and some mortar fire, nothing to
worry about Mom. I guess the NVA aren't baseball
fans is all. Anyway we heard pretty much of it, that
Bob Gibson is something else, watch him Cap
maybe you can pitch like that some day. Seemed
funny to listen to the series anywhere but home
though, seemed like I ought to be sitting in front of
the tv with Dad, and Mom calling us a coupel of
lumps and fixing popcorn. Old Hopkins, he's a real
joker, he scrounged around and got us some pea-

nuts from somewhere and said to make like he's my Mom. I told him it was a good thing my Mom was better looking than him or I'd never got born.

Well that's about it I guess, yall write back, that's what Hopkins says, yall, just like our Texas family, you should hear him.

Love,
Wing

_____

Nov. 22, 1967

Dear Folks,

Happy Thanksgiving, hope you guys are all well and having some good bird. No patrols today, they think we might get a little incoming but that's about it so everybody is having turkey and all, they flew it in special.

Listen I got some good news yesterday, I made Lance Corporal. Some of us took a hill from the NVA last week, I guess that's what did it. I don't know what good it did though, two days later we moved on and the NVA never even bothered to take the hill back. I don't know why anybody wanted it in the first place, sometimes you get crazy things like that around here but anyway I'm glad I made E-3 and all.

Mom I got the cookies they were great, thanks a lot. Hopkins said to tell you your a great cook, that was after he stole some naturly.

Hey Geriatrick, I been meaning to tell you say thanks to Sister for the rosaries, I bet they help, sure couldn't hurt anyway. I still got my medal Dad, its the best.

Love,
Wing

P. S. Hey captain, you ever heard of a lung fish? They got lungs and gills both and when the water goes down and their trapped on land they lie around breathing like humans, its really weird. This has got to be the weirdest place in the world.

Dec. 1, 1967

Dear Wing,

Congratulations on making Lance Corporal! We're all really proud of you. You should hear Mama and Daddy telling everybody, strangers on the street, practically.

I've been pretty busy lately, doing some babysitting for Joey Zatarian while his mother plays in this bridge club she's joined. Joey is Eddie's baby brother, you remember? Only he's not a baby anymore, in fact he's a couple of grades ahead of Dub at school. He's a pretty nice kid, kind of quiet, nothing like Eddie, thank goodness. Just reads comic books, mostly—that's what he's doing now, while I'm writing this letter. Not too bad for fifty cents an hour. Maybe I'll be rich by the next time I see you. I figure all I need is enough to last me till I'm twenty-one—that's when I get the big bucks from the gin game, right?

Mama is all excited because Aunt Margery just sent her a box of pictures and all sorts of things from Nana's house in Beaumont—they've been cleaning out the attic, sounds like. One of the things she sent is this book of poetry by our Great-aunt Geraldine—the one I'm named for, remember? I was kind of excited, too, because my whole life Mama told me that Aunt Geraldine was so great and all, and maybe I would grow up to be smart like her and write books like she did. Only now I'm not so sure about that. The very first line of the first poem is this: "Balboa, Balboa, the Spanish explorer." Daddy says he wants to know should that be pronounced, "Balboa, Balboa, the Spanish explo-ah?" Or is it, "Balborer, Balborer, the Spanish explorer?" So far we can't decide.

Well, I guess that's about all the news I have for now. Stay out of trouble. I mean it.

Love,
Geraldine

P. S. It snowed last week, a pretty nice snow, but it melted already. But Dub says don't worry, he made a giant-size snowball that he's saving for you in the freezer so you can play with it when you get home.

Dec. 15, 1967

Dear Folks,

Well here we are in a place called Khe Sanh, it's the biggest Marine base they got here. It sits down in the middle of a bunch of hills and our guys have some of the hills and the NVA have some and the generals think they want all of them and this base too. So they brought us all up here, the whole Third Battalion, they got us running around on patrols just like before mostly, no big deal Mom.

Hey Captain here's a funny story Hopkins told me, he swears its true. What happened was he was best man at his friends wedding right before he came in-country and anyway he was real nervous at the rehersal dinner because he knew he was going to have to make a speech. And before it was time he left and went to the bathroom and when he got back his friend sitting next to him said hey Hopkins you left your zipper down. So Hopkins said thanks and zipped up and thought boy that was lucky, that would have been embarassing giving his speech like that. So then it got to be time and he stood up and started walking up to the head table to give his speech. And all of a sudden there was this terrible crashing and glasses breaking and food spilling everywhere. And it turns out that old Hopkins had zipped up a part of the tablecloth in his zipper and the whole thing was coming with him. I about died laughing when he told me. When we get home maybe Hopkins can come around and meet you guys some time, I think you'd get a kick out of him.

Well I guess that's all for now, got to catch some zs.

Love,
Wing

Dec. 18, 1967

Dear Geriatrick,

You know it sounds crazy but last night I had a dream that was all green, I mean that was it, just the color green in front of me like a sheet of that construction paper we used to cut out to make chains for the holidays you know? And then I woke up and everything was still green, we were out in the hills and I guess that's why I dreamed it anyway. I mean you can't get away from green around this place, here it is almost Christmas. I know the last time I had to shovel snow I said I hated it but you know I wouldn't mind a white Christmas right about now. But anyway I don't have to shovel snow, guess you guys can have the honor, ha ha.

Well I guess I never wrote you a letter by yourself anyway, I should have on account of all the ones you wrote me. They meant a lot to me, I can tell you that. You know I guess sometimes I'm pretty hard on you but I never meant it that way, I guess I'm just naturly mean. But listen beleive it or not I think your about the best sister anybody ever had. And listen don't worry about what that teacher said about fat cells either, she doesn't know everything and anyway you looked real slim in that last picture Mom sent.

Listen I hope you have a real good Christmas, I wonder if you could do me a favor. You know for the last coupel years I've been going up on the roof and jingling those old slay bells so the Captain would hear the reindeer, so since I wont be there I was thinking maybe you could do it. I mean you'd have to be careful and all but its really not hard or dangerous or anything, all you do is go out my bedroom window to that flat place on the roof over the Cap's room and stamp around some and jingle those bells, nothing to it.

Well I guess that about does it, merry Christmas and all, I'll be thinking about you guys.

Love,
Wing

part three

1968

14

Dear Wing,

Are you okay? We haven't heard from you in a while and everybody's pretty worried; I know probably you've just been busy and had no time to write, that's what Daddy says, anyhow. We listen to the news every night and read all the newspapers we can get—they keep talking about something called a Tet Offensive right around where you said you are, Khe Sanh. It sounds pretty bad, but you're okay, aren't you? Listen, I know you're busy, but if you can get any time at all, please write. Everybody's fine around here, just nervous, is all. I can't think of any news right now; my mind's a blank. Kizzy says woof—that means write soon.

Love,
Geraldine

Feb. 12, 1968

Dear Folks,

Listen I'm really sorry I haven't written but we've been pretty busy like Dad thought. I'm fine, don't worry, the newspapers are probably making it all sound a lot worse than it is, all the action is still pretty much in the hills like it was before. We get some incoming but its not that bad, you sort of get used to when it comes and as long as your ready your okay. Look I'm sorry this is so short but we're pretty busy like I said, I promise I'll write more later. I'm fine really, don't worry Mom.

Love,
Wing

Feb. 12, 1968

Dear Geraldine,

Take this letter someplace private and read it by yourself, its not for anybody else.

We got in a fire fight a coupel weeks ago trying to take back another one of these frigging hills and Hopkins got blown away, he's gone. Listen don't tell Mom, she would just worry, just lose this letter after you read it or burn it or something okay? Maybe I shouldn't write you either but I felt like I ought to tell somebody, somebody ought to know about Hopkins, he was a real good guy. I don't

know, sometimes I get down and then I wonder if
it's all worth it, I mean it doesn't seem like we're
getting anywhere just sitting here rotting and guys
like Hopkins getting blown away and for what. I
guess maybe Dad felt like that in Guadle Canal and
all and he still did his job, I'm trying to do the
same but I don't think this war is much like that
other one. I mean its nothing like John Wayne or
any of that, maybe Sam was right all along, I don't
know. They tell me I'll probably make corporal
now. Funny, Hopkins and me had a bet going about
who would make it first, I guess I win but it doesn't
seem so important now, winning I mean.

Listen I'm okay, I just wanted you to know about
Hopkins so you'd remember him, is all. Now you
know so go tear this up or burn it or whatever.
Thanks.

Love,
Wing

⸺⸺⸺⸺

"Hail Mary, full of grace, the Lord is with
thee. . . ."

Geraldine knelt alone in the church. It was cool
and dim; the only light the flickering of the small red
votive candles, the sanctuary lamp glowing by the
altar, the pools of color spilling from the stained glass
windows. It moved, this colored light, shifting with

the breeze that tossed the branches of the trees outside.

There was a holy smell here. Geraldine supposed it was just a combination of old incense and candle wax and the varnish that Leon the janitor used on the pews, the woodwork. She was sure that's all it was, really. But when she was younger she used to think it was the smell of God—solemn and powerful—and yet comforting, somehow. She had always felt safe here. In the olden days, the sisters had taught her, people would come to the church for protection. People fleeing from mortal enemies would come to the church and cry, "Sanctuary!" and no one was allowed to harm them. But that was a long time ago. Geraldine had read only last week that in Vietnam a whole churchful of people was burned to the ground by Communist guerillas.

She took out Wing's letter and looked at it again. She read it through once more, then began folding it over and over, making it smaller, smaller, wishing she could make it disappear altogether. Not just the paper, but the words. She knew she could always burn the paper, but it wouldn't matter; she could never burn the words—they were stuck in her head forever, now. Poor Hopkins. Poor old Hopkins. Geraldine had never heard his first name. But she would remember him, all right.

"Blessed art thou amongst women, and blessed is the fruit of thy womb, Jesus. . . ."

She was kneeling on the right side of the com-
munion rail, before the statue of the Blessed Virgin.
She had always loved this statue, though she had
feared it, too, a little. When she was younger she
thought that it might come alive and talk to her—
such miracles were always happening to saints in stories. Sometimes she was quite sure that the statue
smiled more broadly one day than another, or tilted
its head just the tiniest bit whenever she blinked.
"You moved, didn't you?" she would pray then, half-
fascinated, half-terrified, and wait for the divine message that was bound to follow.

Poor Hopkins. Poor Wing. That was why he hadn't
written for a while. It wasn't that he was busy; he was
too upset. What was it that he said—that maybe Sam
was right about the war, after all? He was just going
through a bad time because he was so sad about his
friend, right? He hadn't changed his mind about Sam,
had he? This was the first time he had even mentioned
Sam's name since the night they'd fought, way last
summer. Poor Wing. Poor old Wing.

"Holy Mary, Mother of God, pray for us sinners.
. . ." When Geraldine was younger, she had been
terrified of sinning—of "falling into sin"—that was
how they said it in prayers and catechism class. That
was the part that really scared her—the falling part.
She used to think it must be something like falling
into the cellar, that sin was dark and creepy and full
of snakes. Wing had said in one of his letters that the

nights in Vietnam were so dark you couldn't see your hand in front of your face, the darkest nights in the world. . . .

"Pray for us sinners, now and at the hour of our death, Amen." The hour of our death. Poor Hopkins. Poor Wing. Geraldine took two quarters out of her purse and put them in the metal donations box beneath the votive candles. The clinking sound they made seemed loud in the quiet. She picked up a long, thin taper that lay alongside the box, lit it from one of the little flickering candles, and passed its flame to two others. Now two new lights were shining, here in the dusky church. One for Hopkins, one for Wing. It wasn't much. Geraldine knew it wasn't very much. But she didn't know what else to do.

Mon., April 8, 1968

Dear Folks,

Well how's everybody? I am doing fine, thanks for all the letters you guys have been sending, their great. That was a real good joke Captain, that one about the chicken. Some of the guys around here are jelous, they say why the heck does Brennan get all the letters? I tell them just lucky I guess.

I can't beleive some of the news lately, that's something about Martin Luther King getting shot, kind of makes you sick. And what about Johnson saying he's not going to run next year, that was a

surprize. Well maybe it will do some good, him
saying there will be peace talks and all. I'll beleive
it when I see it but I hope so even though you can't
tell any difference around here so far. But anyway
I'm getting short, that means I don't have much
time left in this place Captain, on Easter I'll have 97
more days and a wakeup, not bad.

Well tough going for the Knicks, maybe next
year but anyway its pretty nice weather around here
for a change, blue skies and all and not raining or
hot either one. I guess its just about spring back
home, that means baseball season right Dad? Hey
Captain you better get out that mit and get it oiled
up, I bet Dad will hit you some grounders if the
weathers good. Listen I might take my R & R
pretty soon, I was all ready due for it a coupel
months ago but some of the guys say its better to
take it when your short, then the time goes faster
after that and anyway its better luck. You get kind
of supersticious about things like that around here.

Well I guess that's about it, maybe the next letter
you get from me will come from Australia or someplace, then not long after that and I'll be home.
That sounds good, home I mean.

Love,
Wing

"Look here, Geraldine—here's how to make the best ones—first you dip 'em a while in red, then green, then purple, then yellow—"

"Good grief, Dub—not in the yellow—not after all those other colors—you'll turn the yellow to orange or something!"

"Well, that's okay. I like orange."

"But then we won't have any more yellow. Mama, tell him."

"Hmm?" Mama was sitting at the kitchen table with them, answering Wing's most recent letter. With one hand she was writing; with the other she was turning an egg around and around in a cup filled with fizzy blue dye. This was going to be a really blue egg. Today was Holy Saturday, the day before Easter, the day the Brennans always dyed their eggs. Kizzy was lying on the floor at Dub's feet, hoping he would drop another one—she had already eaten two. The smell of hard-boiled eggs and vinegar, of countless other Easters, was strong in the kitchen air. Every now and again a whiff of early spring broke through. It was a fine day, one of the first really warm days they'd had so far, and Daddy had put up the screen on the storm door to let the fresh air inside. He was out back himself, puttering around in the vegetable garden. Geraldine could hear him singing from all the way in here:

"In your Easter bonnet,
With all the frills upon it . . ."

"Mama—"

Mama looked up now. "What is it, Geraldine? Oh, no, Dub—don't put that purple egg in the yellow, honey—it'll turn the yellow orange or something."

"That's what I was trying to tell him."

Dub sighed. "But it was going to be my masterpiece!"

Mama smiled. "Your masterpiece? Well, now, we certainly don't want to stand in the way of art! Tell you what, Captain, just let us finish up a couple more yellow ones, and then you can do whatever you want with the yellow dye—how's that?"

"I guess that would be all right," Dub said, smiling back at Mama.

"Let's see now," she said. "How many of these have we broken so far? We have to keep count of all the eggs—we don't want to miss finding one like we did that other time."

"I remember that," Geraldine said, making a face. "That was awful—remember, Dub? We thought it was a dead rat or something, and then two months later Wing found that old egg under the couch in the living room. Phew!"

Dub laughed, and Mama said, "Now, don't you go telling that story outside this family—it doesn't exactly paint me as the ideal housekeeper!" But she was laughing, too.

"Aw, Mama, you're a great housekeeper—rotten eggs are better than dead rats, any day!" Geraldine said.

"Where's that white Crayola?" Dub asked. "I've still got to write our names on some of these eggs."

"Well, you had it just a minute ago when you were drawing that rabbit," Geraldine reminded him. "What'd you do with it after that?"

"I laid it right there on the edge of the table. Kizzy, you didn't eat it, did you?"

"Kizzy wouldn't do a thing like that—she's too smart to eat a Crayola, aren't you, Kizzy?" Geraldine said.

As if in answer, Kizzy perked up her ears, hauled herself to her feet, and lumbered out of the kitchen, barking.

"Now, look what you've done—you've hurt her feelings," Geraldine said to Dub, and then she heard the sound of heavy footsteps on the front porch.

"No, I didn't—it's someone at the door, that's all," Dub said. "I'll get it." He raced off after Kizzy, just as the knocking began. Kizzy was still barking, louder now.

"You'd better go quiet her down and see who it is, honey," Mama said. "I'd go, but I'm a mess—all over vinegar. Listen, if it's that meat man again, tell him we just can't afford to buy from him this month."

"Yes, ma'am." Geraldine didn't bother to mention that she was pretty vinegary herself. She figured the meat man wouldn't care. "Kizzy, you hush!" she called, on her way through the dining room. "Leave him alone, Kiz—"

The words died on her lips. Dub had opened the

front door already. Standing just outside on the porch, caps in hand, were two Marine officers.

Dub looked up at her, smiling. "They're Marines, like Wing. They want to talk to Mama and Daddy." He beamed at the officers. "Do you know my brother? He's a corporal now, Corporal A. Wing Brennan, Jr."

"Mama," Geraldine tried to call. Her lungs were airless, useless. "Mama—" She couldn't move.

"What is it, Geraldine?" Mama came into the dining room, wiping her hands on her apron. "Is it Mr. Marcella again?" And then she saw the officers too, and her face changed; she went very still and white, and for a second it looked as if she were going to cry. But she didn't cry. She took a deep breath and walked to the door. "Geraldine," she said, "take Dub and Kizzy out to the garden, please, and tell your daddy I need him." She turned back to the Marines. "I'm sorry about the dog, gentlemen," she apologized. "Won't you come in?"

15

The house had never been so quiet. Dub had cried himself to sleep hours ago, with Kizzy at the foot of his bed. And finally Daddy had taken Mama to bed, too; Geraldine was glad of that—she was worried about her. Mama had stayed so very still since the soldiers left, sat so very silently at the kitchen table while Daddy told Dub and Geraldine how Wing had been hit by a mortar shell on a hill outside Khe Sanh on Thursday morning, and died that night without regaining consciousness. Dub wouldn't believe it at first.

"No," he had insisted, "Wing wouldn't die—they must have got him mixed up with somebody else." But gradually he was made to understand, and then his tears came. Daddy held him in his arms and cried, too—Daddy, who never cried, who always laughed and sang and talked too loud—while Mama, who must have spilled gallons of tears in the last year, who cried at dog-food commercials, Mama just sat there, staring into space, twirling that little wire egg dipper in her fingers. Geraldine sat staring, too, her insides numb, frozen solid like the lump of snow that Dub had been saving in the freezer for the past four months. At last Dub had tired himself out, and Daddy carried him to bed. He came back to the table to sit with Mama and Geraldine, then asked if he could get them something to eat—would they like him to pick up some chicken, maybe? But Mama had said not to bother. . . .

"I'll fix some supper in a little while," she said, "just as soon as I see to a few things. I've got to get the rest of these eggs dyed, and then I really ought to—" She had stopped, looked stricken.

"Ought to what, sweetheart?" Daddy asked gently. "Is there something I can do for you?"

"I was just going to say," she said, with a catch in her voice, "I was going to say that I ought to finish my letter to Wing—" And then she began to sob, too, and Daddy held her, the way he had held Dub, and let her cry and cry. For a long time afterward they sat at the table, talking quietly about Wing, about how when he was newborn they had nicknamed him "The Judge" because he was so serious looking; how when he was four he wouldn't let them tie his balloon to his wrist at the fair because everyone would think he was a "little kid"; how at ten he had begged so to keep the fat black mongrel that Mama had called Kismet, meaning fate, when it followed him home one snowy day. Small memories that turned and twisted inside Geraldine. They made her ache, for together they added up to Wing and nobody else.

Someone put food in front of her; she ate it automatically. It could have been sand. And then a while later Daddy asked if she wasn't tired. Didn't she want to go to bed?

"In a little," she told him.

"Are you all right, honey?" Mama asked, and she tried to hug Geraldine.

"I'm fine," she answered, pulling away. "I just want to sit here, okay—can't I just sit here by myself for a while?"

Mama and Daddy looked at each other, but they didn't say anything after that, just good night, then squeezed Geraldine's stiff shoulders and kissed her stony cheek and went up to bed. . . .

That was about half an hour ago. And still Geraldine was sitting, staring into space. She had been sitting so long her legs were asleep. Little by little it had come to her what this feeling was, stuck somewhere between her stomach and her throat, this lump of burning ice, this aching without tears. She was mad, that's what it was. She was mad at Wing for dying. He didn't have to go to Vietnam. He wasn't drafted—he volunteered, for crying out loud, he went to a lot of trouble to get himself killed, quitting school just when his grades were looking better. It was his own fault, his own stupid fault.

But not his fault alone.

Geraldine picked up the salt shaker and began pouring salt in a pile on the table.

Sure, Wing went to the war of his own free will,

but he didn't start it—it was already there, waiting for him. So now he was gone, he was dead, she was mad at him but it didn't do her any good. She couldn't yell at him or punch him in the nose or even write him a letter, anymore. And whose fault was that?

The salt shaker was empty now. With the tip of her index finger, Geraldine began making roads in the pile, circular roads starting in the middle and growing wider and wider.

God's fault, maybe. He was to blame for the whole world being so fouled up, wasn't He? The sisters said He had created everything—that meant all the troublemakers, too, right? Nobody asked Him; nobody asked for Communists or peace freaks or low-down dirty snakes in the grass like—

Like Sam.

Geraldine stopped drawing in the salt. She sat very still.

It was Sam's fault that Wing was dead.

Sam, the traitor. It was all Sam's fault.

Geraldine stared at the mess she had made. She was madder than she'd ever been in her life, but it was a different kind of mad than she'd felt before this day—not the kind that made her want to scream and kick somebody. This was a colder, stonier fury that left her strangely calm.

Slowly, painstakingly, she swept the salt from the table into the palm of her left hand and refilled the shaker, until finally she had every grain back where it belonged. She stood up and stretched her stiff legs, walked upstairs and went to the bathroom, then walked downstairs again. She put on her jacket. It had been warm earlier, but she suspected the night air would be chilly. She opened the door quietly and stepped outside onto the porch.

She was right about the temperature. It felt like football weather, a beautiful night, blacker than black, stabbed with a million stars. Geraldine walked to the barn and swung open the heavy door. Something scurried inside and she froze, shuddering. Then there was no sound but the distant rushing of the swollen stream. She got her bicycle and closed the door. It was downhill, mostly, to the street, then downhill again, more often than not, from the Brennans' house to the Dailys'.

She knew she shouldn't be out at midnight. She didn't care. The Geraldine of this morning would have been afraid, wouldn't have considered it. But this morning was a lifetime ago, and she hardly remembered that other Geraldine. She doubted she'd know her if she met her on the street.

The Zatarians' house was dark. From somewhere within a dog barked as she rode past. Eddie was home now, had come home last month. It didn't seem fair somehow, that Eddie had made it home safely, and not Wing. Wing could always beat Eddie at anything— why not this, the one time it mattered? Geraldine pushed the thought away. It wasn't Eddie she was mad at. She had no quarrel with Eddie.

Here was the Dailys' driveway. She turned in,

parked her bike beside the front steps, walked up to the front door. There was no doorbell, only an old-fashioned knocker. Without giving herself a chance to stop and think, she lifted it and knocked loudly, again and again. A minute later she could hear footsteps inside, see the curtain moving at the window beside the door. "Who's there?" said Mrs. Daily's voice, as the porch light came on.

"It's Geraldine," she answered. The door opened.

"Geraldine? What on earth?" Mrs. Daily looked awful, eyes all puffy from sleep, hair tumbling around her head every which way, a strong dark sleep crease running slant-wise along her left cheek. In some distant part of Geraldine's brain, there was a voice telling her she ought to be sorry for waking her, frightening her in the middle of the night—

"I'm sorry, Mrs. Daily," she heard herself say. "I have to see Sam—he's home for Easter, isn't he?"

Mrs. Daily shook her head. "No, he's not. He was here for a couple of days, but he went back to Washington today—there's some sort of march planned for tomorrow—"

She broke off abruptly, as if she had just remembered to whom she was speaking.

So, thought Geraldine. Another march. She should have known. Sam wasn't here; she had come for nothing. "I'm sorry I bothered you," she said, and she turned to go.

"Geraldine, what's wrong?" Mrs. Daily asked anxiously, following her onto the porch. "What are you doing out by yourself in the middle of the night? Has something happened?"

Geraldine looked at her. Mrs. Daily might as well know, she figured. She'd know soon enough. Geraldine believed she half-knew already. "Wing is dead," she answered, the words cold in her throat.

"Oh, Geraldine. Oh, honey." Mrs. Daily's eyes filled with tears. This bothered Geraldine. Wing wasn't *her* son, *her* brother. She had no right to cry, while Geraldine's eyes were dry. Still, "I'm so sorry," Mrs. Daily was saying now, with the salt water spilling down her cheeks. "Is there anything I can do? Shall I go to your mother?"

"No, ma'am," said Geraldine, shaking her head. "She's asleep. They're all asleep. I'm sorry I bothered you; I thought Sam was here. I'll go home now."

"Not on your bicycle, Geraldine, not at this hour. I'll drive you home—just let me put something on, get my keys—"

"No!" Geraldine practically shouted. She didn't know why—she hadn't intended to shout. Mrs. Daily looked at her, surprised. "No, ma'am," she said, more softly. "No, thank you, I mean. It only takes five minutes on my bike; I'll be home in five minutes." And without waiting for Sam's mother to respond, she ran down the stairs, hopped on her bike, and pedaled away furiously, up the hill.

It was hard work, that uphill climb. By the time she reached her driveway she was sweating under her jacket, panting like a dog. She parked her bike beside the porch steps, walked quietly up to the door, opened it. She paused and listened. No sound. Geraldine walked into the kitchen, took out the phone book, and flipped through the yellow pages until she came to the one she wanted. She scribbled an address on a piece of paper, put that in her pocket. Then she scribbled a note on another piece, Scotch-taped that to the refrigerator door. She tiptoed upstairs to her bedroom and found her wallet. There were nearly thirty-five dollars in it. She had been saving her babysitting money since Christmas to buy Wing a welcome-home present.

She knew what she ought to do. She ought to get in bed, close her eyes, and go to sleep. But she couldn't sleep, couldn't imagine sleeping. There was something she had to do first.

16

"Washington, this stop; Washington D.C.," the bus driver announced.

Geraldine jerked awake again. How long had she been asleep? It seemed she'd been dreaming one dream after another for hours, but when she looked at her watch, only minutes had passed since she'd last checked it.

"Looks like we're here," the woman next to her said cheerfully.

"Yes, ma'am," said Geraldine.

The bus slowed down, pulled into the terminal, and labored to a halt. There was a sighing, hissing sound from the brakes, the choking smell of diesel exhaust— a smell Geraldine associated with grade school, with overheated school buses on cold winter mornings, with Wing's brooding presence behind her on the back seat. . . . She turned, half-expecting to see him. But there was only an old oriental gentleman, who smiled and nodded.

"Are you sure you have everything?" the woman asked now.

"Yes, ma'am." Around them, other passengers were putting on coats, lifting bags from the overhead rack. Geraldine had nothing with her to collect but her jacket and her wallet containing two dollars and sixty-five cents and the other half of her round-trip ticket. She hadn't come to stay.

The woman looked concerned. "Do you see that boyfriend of yours yet? I don't want to leave you alone until you see him."

Dutifully, Geraldine looked out the window. "Yes, ma'am, he's out there," she said. Nothing to it, this lying.

The woman breathed a sigh. "Well, all right then— you enjoy your trip. Don't forget to look for those cherry blossoms!"

"I won't," Geraldine said. And then the woman was gone, squeezing her way down the crowded aisle to the open door. Geraldine waited until she was safely out of sight, then followed.

The terminal was old and smelled sour, of stale cigarette smoke and unwashed bodies. It was crowded with people of every description, men with slick hair and shiny shoes, soldiers with duffel bags and shaved heads, frazzled-looking mothers with crying children in tow. A bearded boy and a girl with yellow braids were giving out limp-looking daisies to all takers— there weren't many—and saying "Peace" to anybody who would listen; not many would. Geraldine avoided them as if they were contaminated and walked to the other side of the room, where she had spied a rackful of travel brochures beside a dingy candy counter. She needed a map of Washington.

"That will be twenty-five cents, please," said a white-haired man who appeared behind the counter just as Geraldine found what she wanted. She shelled out the quarter.

"Could you please show me," she asked the man, "where we are on this map?"

"Glad to," the man answered, taking the map from Geraldine and unfolding it. "We're right here, corner of Twelfth and New York. Where is it you want to go?"

"The White House," Geraldine said. She figured if there was a peace march anywhere in Washington, that would be the place. She had seen marches time and again on the seven o'clock news. That was where she'd find Sam, surely.

"Oh, well, that's easy—you're almost there. Just go straight out this door—that's New York Avenue right out there—then turn to your right and follow New York about three blocks till it turns into Pennsylvania, and there's the White House on your left, easy as pie."

"Thank you," said Geraldine, relieved that it sounded simple. She started to walk away.

"You'll need to turn left on Executive if you want the tourist entrance," the man called after her. "But

I don't think that's open on Easter Sunday, sweetie —the egg rolling's not till tomorrow."

Geraldine nodded her thanks again and walked out the door to New York Avenue. Easter, she thought dully. She had forgotten it. She passed a large church—New York Avenue Presbyterian Church, she read on a sign. People were coming out now, little girls in beribboned hats and frilly dresses, boys in sailor suits, smiling parents. Geraldine supposed she should have gone to Mass, but Mass had been the farthest thing from her mind this morning, and now it was too late, after one p.m. She wondered if anybody had remembered to hide the eggs at home. Or if Dub had had the heart to look for them. Her own heart clenched into a fist as she thought of Dub and his grief. Angrily, she squared her shoulders and walked on.

An immense gray building loomed across the street. U. S. DEPARTMENT OF THE TREASURY, she saw. Geraldine crossed East Executive, ignoring the arrrows that pointed to the tourist entrance; she hadn't come here as a tourist. Now New York Avenue became Pennsylvania—and that was the White House, wasn't it, through those trees? Sixteen hundred Pennsylvania Avenue—that must be it.

The weather was even warmer than yesterday. Geraldine took off her jacket as she walked along a sidewalk crowded with people laughing, calling to one another, snapping photographs. A man with a headband reading MAKE LOVE NOT WAR played a guitar on the corner. Knots of people formed around him, pausing for a minute to listen, then trickling away to other streets, other sights. Sam was not among them.

Here was the front gate. Geraldine peered through and saw the White House clearly now, looking so much like a picture postcard that she almost didn't believe in it. The whole day, the whole city seemed unreal, as if she were still riding the bus, trapped in another dream. She wished she were. She wished she would wake up and find that the whole last year and a half had been a dream, and Wing would be at home, laughing at her for believing in nightmares.

Geraldine turned away from the White House gate and scanned the faces in the sidewalk crowd once more. Sam was nowhere to be seen. Here was at least one protester, though—a girl with long, straight hair and granny glasses. She was walking in Geraldine's direction, carrying a sign that said, PRESIDENT THIEU IS A FASCIST PIG! Had to be a friend of Sam's, Geraldine figured. She waited until the girl was closer, then spoke up. "Excuse me, do you know a guy named Sam Daily?"

The girl shook her head. "No," she said. "Does he go to Catholic U?"

"No, Georgetown."

"Oh, well, I probably wouldn't know him then."

"Oh. Well, thanks." Geraldine turned away, then back again. "Have you heard if there's a demonstration planned for today?"

"Not that I know of—but there's always something going on. You might try over by the Washington Monument. Sometimes they start over there."

"All right, thanks."

At the Monument a boy in moccasins and love beads sent her across the Mall to the Capitol; at the Capitol a slender black woman in a shawl suggested she try the Lincoln Memorial; at the Lincoln Memorial two white-robed girls with flowers in their hair told her to check the Jefferson Memorial. And all the while that sense of unreality was growing stronger. Washington was beautiful, she could see that, but she was only vaguely aware of its dignified buildings and wide avenues and cherry trees blossoming beside blue water. Seeing, she did not see, as she passed through temples dedicated to great men and their principles: "We hold these truths to be self-evident, that all men are created equal, that they are endowed by their Creator with certain unalienable Rights . . ." ". . . that government of the people, by the people, for the people, shall not perish from the earth." She had wandered, somehow, between the covers of her history book, or into that old movie that came on television sometimes, "Mr. Smith Goes to Washington." This wasn't real; this wasn't happening. Come on, Wing, she almost said aloud, joke's over; I'm waiting—tell me this isn't happening—

At the Jefferson Memorial a boy wearing a T-shirt that said *Hell No, We Won't Go* told her she should try the Washington Monument again. "I heard something about a candlelight march tonight," he said. "I'm probably going over there myself in a minute. I've got a motorcycle—you want a ride?"

Geraldine backed away from him. "No, thanks—I like walking," she lied. Her feet were killing her, but she wasn't about to get on a motorcycle with some strange hippie. She started walking again. By now it was nearly six o'clock. She had planned to find Sam, say what she had to say, and then take a six-thirty bus back home. She knew she ought to go back to the bus station, knew her parents were worrying—furious, probably. She had told them the truth in her note, told them where she was going, but she had also said that she would come home tonight. . . . If she missed that six-thirty bus, there was no telling when the next one left. Still, she couldn't leave without finding Sam. He had to be here somewhere, and now it looked as if she were finally on the right track. She wasn't leaving. Not yet.

Somewhere in the distance a siren wailed. It grew louder, approaching, then faded away. Geraldine crossed herself, as the sisters had taught her to do whenever she heard the sound of someone's trouble, to pray for God's mercy on that unknown soul. She did it without thinking, a reflex action, like the time she'd become confused and genuflected in the aisle at the movie theater. She wasn't thinking about anything but finding Sam; she was afraid of what might happen if she let herself think of anything else.

The sun was setting to her left, a perfect red circle

in a rose-colored haze. Across the Tidal Pool, the Washington Monument pointed, glowing, to the sky, the white dome of the Capitol floated in the gathering darkness. It was getting chilly again. Her breath was visible now in the arc of the street lamp she was passing. She put on her jacket once more.

Now she was nearing the green where the Monument stood, and her heart began to race. The boy must have been right about the march, for a crowd had gathered since Geraldine had been here earlier—a jostling, murmuring throng. There were people everywhere—all kinds of people, but young mostly. Many of them were carrying placards about peace and love and brotherhood. This was it, surely—this must be it. Someone here would know Sam.

"Excuse me, do you know Sam Daily? Excuse me, excuse me. . . ."

A few of the people merely shook their heads and turned away, but many more were kind—smiling people who tried to help. Geraldine hardened her heart against their kindness; these were all the enemy, she told herself—Wing's enemies. They might look kind on the outside, but underneath they were cold-blooded killers, cowards.

"Excuse me, do you know Sam Daily? Excuse me."

"What's the matter, little sister? Did you lose somebody?" It was a sweet-faced black woman, maybe fifty or so. She carried a sign that said, BRING OUR BOYS HOME ALIVE. The words stabbed at Geraldine; this woman must have a son over there, a boy like Wing.

Geraldine turned away, thinking of Mama, bitterness rising again in her throat. "Sam Daily," she muttered. "I'm looking for Sam Daily."

"Did you say Daily?" a voice asked behind her. Geraldine turned and saw a man in a wheelchair. He was wearing a beat-up army jacket.

"Yes, sir," she answered, feeling confused. This man must have been in combat, then; he had lost both his legs. She couldn't very well think of *him* as the enemy, could she? What was he doing here, anyway?

"Fella named Sam Daily was the one called our group about tonight," the veteran said. "I talked to him when I first got here—he's around somewhere. Hold on a second, I'll find him for you."

And before Geraldine had a chance to wonder how on earth he was going to manage in a wheelchair when she had failed all day long with two good legs, the man set up a cry: "Daily! Sam Daily! Anybody seen a guy named Daily?" And in a second someone else took it up, and then another, and another; it rolled around the crowd like retreating thunder. And then after a while Geraldine could hear another sound coming back, answering: "Over here . . . Daily's over here . . . this way . . . this way . . ." And the next thing she knew she was being passed along the trail of that sound, from one person to another. Hands were pushing her gently, pulling, nudging; she was being tugged along, borne as if on the crest of a wave, handed from one to another until she reached the very foot of the Monument.

And there was Sam. He was kneeling beside a big cardboard box, handing out candles, laughing at something or other with the people around him. He looked good. Great, even. Wing was dead and Sam was laughing, looking great. For a moment Geraldine couldn't speak; she was choked by the unfairness of everything.

"Hey, Daily," said a voice at her left ear. "Somebody here looking for you."

Sam looked up. His face changed. "Geraldine?" he said, standing.

"Yeah," she answered, forcing her voice to cooperate.

He came closer, smiling again now, put his hand on her arm. At his touch, an involuntary shudder ran through her. "I can't believe it," he was saying. "This is great—what are you doing in Washington? Are your parents here?"

So he didn't know yet. His mother hadn't called him, Geraldine supposed, or maybe she had called, and he hadn't been home. Geraldine was glad. She wanted to be the one to tell him. She hoped she would hurt him. She shook her head. "No," she said, "just me. I came on the bus—I came to see you. I've been looking for you all day."

"Really?" Sam looked puzzled. "I'm sorry, I wish I'd known you were coming. I could have met your bus. Say, how's all your family? What do you hear from Wing?"

Now, she told herself. Now was the time to tell him. Now was when she was supposed to say that

Wing was dead; he's dead, she should say, and it's your fault, Sam—you killed him. Say it, she told herself. That's what you came all this way to say—

But the words wouldn't come. For some reason she wanted to put off the moment, as if not saying the words would keep Wing alive, in a way—even if only in Sam's mind, even if only for a little while, even if it didn't matter at all. So what she heard herself saying was, "We got a letter from him yesterday; he says the weather's been pretty good, he says maybe he'll take his R & R in Australia. . . ."

Just then someone, somewhere, must have given a signal, because for a moment the crowd's murmuring was hushed, and a chant began to rise from the darkness all around. At first Geraldine couldn't understand what the voices were saying, but then the words grew stronger, clearer: "Peace, give us peace. . . ." Like words of prayer, words fit for church—solemn and sad and beautiful—"Peace, give us peace. . . ."

"He says it's green at Christmastime, he says they have fish with lungs, he says we ought to get the mitt oiled up . . ."

Now the couple next to Geraldine—the man was balding and bearded, the woman expecting a baby— this couple struck a match and lit a candle, and passed its light to a girl beside them, and she passed it on to the man next to her. And suddenly there were candles burning everywhere, a million tiny flames dancing all around Sam and Geraldine, and again she thought of church, and words from the gospel—"And the light shineth in darkness; and the darkness comprehended it not."

"He says his friend Hopkins got blown away, he says maybe you were right about the war, he says he liked Dub's joke about the chicken—" And now tears were streaming down her face, the tears she had thought would never come. I'm doing this all wrong, she thought frantically. What's the matter with me, anyhow? This wasn't what I meant to say—

The lights were moving, shifting into a sort of ragged line, and the line of lights began to form a circle around the Monument.

"Geraldine," Sam was saying gently, "Geraldine, what's wrong?" But she was sobbing now, she couldn't speak. And so Sam put his arm around her shoulders, and led her off to the side a little, and sat her down. He sat beside her, with his arms around her, holding her, their backs pressed against the cold marble of the Monument's base.

"Peace," said the voices, "give us peace. . . ."

For a long time they sat there. Or maybe it wasn't so long—ten minutes, an hour—Geraldine didn't know. She had lost all sense of time. They sat there while the lights moved off in the direction of the White House and the voices grew fainter. And gradually her sobbing diminished, too.

"It's Wing, isn't it?" Sam said quietly. "Wing's dead."

Geraldine nodded. She never had to say it; Sam had said it for her. She had thought she only wanted to hurt him, and he was hurt. She knew that. But she had been wrong; this wasn't what she wanted, after all.

The procession was far away now, the flickering of the candles lost among all the other lights of the city.

"Your friends left without you," Geraldine said at last.

"It doesn't matter," Sam said dully. "We were too late, anyhow."

17

It was nearing four in the morning when Geraldine opened her eyes and saw the lights of the Tappan Zee Bridge shining on the black waters of the Hudson, far below. The eastern sky ahead held just the faintest suggestion of dawn. Geraldine sat up straighter, glanced across the borrowed Ford's green vinyl upholstery at Sam. Silent Sam. He had said next to nothing since they left the Beltway Coffee Shop outside Washington nearly six hours ago. He had made her eat a hamburger there, and drink a glass of milk.

"I'm not hungry," she had said, but he'd ordered it for her anyway, then called her father on the pay phone in the corner and told him that Geraldine was all right, that he had borrowed a friend's car and was bringing her home. All of which had made her feel about two years old, though she didn't mind that much, really. She was too tired to mind, tired of thinking, glad to let somebody else figure everything out. Her brain felt thick, stupid, as if it had been wrapped in layers of wool.

"Was he very mad?" she asked, once Sam was sitting across from her at the formica-topped table.

"I guess," he said. He looked as exhausted as she felt.

"I'm sorry if he yelled at you," Geraldine said. It was an effort to make her tongue form the words. "I guess he was worried. He always gets mad when he's worried."

"It doesn't matter," Sam said, and he shook his head as if to say nothing mattered anymore.

He hadn't said a word further, except to ask for the check when Geraldine finished eating. After the first bite she had found, to her surprise, that she *was* hungry, starving, really. But Sam had taken only coffee.

And then they had climbed back into the green Ford and driven in silence for hours and hours, and Geraldine had slept, sort of, until the bridge.

"How're you feeling?" Sam asked, seeing her stir.

"All right," she answered. It wasn't exactly true, but it wasn't exactly a lie, either. She didn't think there was a word for the way she was feeling. She was going home; that was all that mattered. Sam was taking her home. Or she was taking *him* home; that was really closer to the truth, wasn't it? And deep down, the reason she had come all this way? To find Sam, to bring him back home again. Strange, how much clearer some things were at four o'clock in the morning.

"Are *you* all right?" she asked him now, though she doubted he would tell if he weren't.

Sam didn't answer right away. Geraldine had decided he wasn't going to answer at all, when he began to speak quietly. "The last time I saw my father," he said, "I threw up all over his uniform. I don't remember it. I was only two years old. But Mom told me— I don't know why, exactly. Maybe she thought it was funny, some way. Or maybe she was mad—I really don't remember." Sam was quiet for a minute, staring straight ahead at the road. "He wasn't a hero or anything," he continued after a while. "Mom taught me to call him that, but it isn't true, not really. The way he died—it was a mistake, that's all, just bad luck. He wasn't even on duty—just riding back from a weekend pass in some jeep, and the driver made a wrong turn and ended up on this bridge that was scheduled to get blown up just then. A big mistake, that's all it was."

Geraldine felt that she ought to say something, but nothing seemed right. And then after another little while, Sam started talking again. "When I was a kid I used to have this dream—a sort of daydream, you know, where I'd be riding with my dad in the jeep that day. And he'd be telling jokes, like the ones in his letters—Mom has every one of them, still. And I'd be laughing, but only kind of half-listening, because I'd be reading the map. And pretty soon the driver would get confused—turn left when he ought to turn right. But I would notice in the nick of time —'Not that way,' I'd say. 'We don't want that bridge; it's not safe.' And Dad would say, 'Nice going, son—

that was a close call, wasn't it? Good thing for me you were here.' " Sam let out a long breath. "That was my dream. But what I really did was throw up on his uniform."

"You were just a baby," Geraldine said. "You couldn't help it."

Sam shook his head. "I have this talent for endings, I guess. The last time I saw Wing, I punched him in the face. And then he broke my nose."

"Because you were a protester?"

"Because I told him he was crazy to go back to the Marines after his leave, because I told him I'd heard there were guys who could help him get to Canada. I'd asked around, found out how he could do it. Told him he'd have to be stupid not to try. That made him mad, I guess. So he called me gutless, and then I started punching. And somewhere in there he broke my nose."

"So that's what happened that day," Geraldine said.

"That's what happened," said Sam.

The two of them were quiet again until the car turned right down the road where they both lived, then right once more, into the Brennans' driveway.

Yellow light streamed from every window. Mama and Daddy appeared on the porch before Sam had turned the motor off. They must have been waiting all night, Geraldine realized, the way they had waited for Wing that other time.

Now she was opening her door. And Sam was opening his, and getting out; he meant to face them, she saw. Together, they made the long walk up to the porch steps. Sam stopped there, but Geraldine kept going.

"Thank God you're all right," Mama said, when she had Geraldine safe in her arms. "We were so frightened—you won't ever do that again, will you, darling? You won't ever run away again."

"I didn't run away," Geraldine tried to say. "It wasn't that."

Daddy had his hands on her shoulders now, holding on tightly. "Never mind," he said. "We'll talk about it later, after you've rested." He turned to Sam now, who was standing a little way off still, at the edge of the porch. Geraldine thought Daddy was going to say something to him; he cleared his throat, as if to prepare. But he only shook his head and shrugged his shoulders a little, in a way that Geraldine had seen Wing shrug his a thousand times. And then he turned from him.

"Thank you for bringing our child home, Sam," Mama said, and then she turned, too; both Geraldine's parents were turning away from Sam, drawing Geraldine with them into the house. She looked back. Sam stood for a minute, and then began walking toward the green Ford.

And as Geraldine watched him go, it struck her suddenly that he was going forever, that she was losing Sam, too, just as she had lost Wing.

She broke away from her parents—"*Wait*, Sam!" she was shouting now; it wasn't yet five in the morning, but she didn't care. "Tell them!" she shouted, but Sam didn't seem to understand her. "He was only trying to help Wing, all along," she said to Daddy; she was crying again, but she scarcely noticed. "He was doing it all for Wing, the whole time, trying to end the war before he got hurt, don't you see? Please come back, Sam! Tell them the truth—tell them you loved him, too—"

18

"Eternal rest grant unto him, O Lord, and let perpetual light shine upon him. May his soul, and the souls of all the faithful departed, rest in peace. Amen."

It was May now, and Wing had come home, too. The old cemetery near the church was overflowing with family and friends; there was a Marine Honor Guard, Uncle Wallace and all Mama's Texas relatives, Mrs. Daily, the Zatarians, Sister Magdalena and Sister Mary Margaret and all the nuns from the grade school and high school; Wing's classmates as well—Maureen O'Donnell, the guys from the basketball team, even Phil Rawlings . . .

And Sam.

"It seems strange," he said, when Monsignor Holub had finished the prayer and nodded for him to begin, "to think of Wing resting. I never knew him to rest much—to sit still, even, for more than five minutes at a stretch. Nobody had half his energy. 'Just one more game,' he'd say, when the rest of us were ready to drop. Nobody ever tried harder. There wasn't much time—I guess there's never enough time. But I wouldn't take a hundred years with anyone else for the seven I had with Wing. He was my friend. He'll always be my friend."

And when it was over, after the Marines had fired their guns in Wing's honor and played taps, after they had folded the flag from the coffin and given it to Mama, Daddy went to Sam. He offered him his hand, and Sam took it. "Thank you, son," he said.

"Come on, Dub. You've been up there for over an hour."

"I like it up here, okay? I'm never coming down."

"Never? You're going to get pretty hungry, living in a tree."

"I don't care. Look, you don't have to hang around if you don't want to. Just go on home and leave me alone."

The Lover's Tree was in bloom again. Dub sat high in its branches, glowering down at Kizzy and Geraldine. He had disappeared about an hour ago, and Mama sent Geraldine looking. She'd had a hunch she'd find him here. He was escaping—she understood that; the house was still teeming with funeral guests.

"Please come down, Dub. You make me nervous, up so high. I don't want to leave you here by yourself, and Mama's waiting."

"Is that Eddie Zatarian still at the house?"

"I don't know—I guess so—why?"

"Because he makes me sick, that's why. I'm not going back while he's there."

"Why? What did he do?"

"It's not what he did—it's what he said. He didn't know I was listening, but I heard him, all right. He was bragging about how he made it back safe from Nam because he passed some smartness test and got a desk job. Just like he didn't think Wing was smart or something."

"Oh, Dub, he didn't mean that; he was just pumping himself up, that's all—he wasn't thinking about Wing. Eddie's brain can't hold more than one thought at a time, anyway."

"Well, I don't care. He makes me sick. Next time I see him, I'm gonna punch him right in the nose."

"Well, I doubt you'll be seeing much of him, living up there with the birds."

"That's okay with me."

"Look, if you don't come down, I'm going to have to come up there and get you."

"No, you won't, either. You *hate* being high up— you're too scared of falling."

"Oh, yeah?"

"Yeah."

"Sez who?"

"Sez me."

"You think I'm chicken?"

"That's what I said."

"Okay, Dub—I really mean it now—are you coming down, or am I coming up?"

"You come up—I dare you."

"You dare me?"

"I double, triple, quadruple dare you!"

"All right, then, here I come."

"Ha!"

The "ha!" did it. Geraldine took a deep breath, got a toehold on the lowest available nail—which wasn't any too low—then took a death grip on another. Just take it easy, she told herself. One step at a time, easy does it, now—higher, higher—that's it, nothing to it, right? Just don't look down, that's all—keep your eyes on where you're going—

She looked down. Kizzy was wagging her tail, smiling her dog smile at Geraldine, her paws on the trunk of the tree. The ground was a hundred miles away. Geraldine's stomach did a somersault. The world was tilting. She froze.

"Hey, Geraldine, you're doing great! Don't stop now—you're almost here." Dub's tone had changed all at once; Geraldine figured he had never thought she'd get this far. Go on, she told herself. You can do it—go on—show him you can do it. She was moving again now, one foot at a time, her face pressed so close to the scarred gray bark that she could smell its good woody smell, taste it, almost. One foot at a time—higher, higher—

"You made it!" Dub cried. "Hey, way to go, Geraldine—you did it!"

"I did, didn't I?" She was sitting on the branch

beside Dub, holding on for dear life. Just then Kizzy started barking, and there was the sound of feet tramping through the underbrush beneath the tree.

"Hey, guys!" a voice called. "You up there?"

It was Sam.

Geraldine looked down through the trembling red leaves and fragile blossoms and saw his face, and for a split second she was six years old, and Wing was somewhere just behind, or ahead, running through the woods with a water balloon, playing war. . . .

And then she remembered where she was, *when* she was, and the years fell back in place, heavy as stones.

"Hey, Sam," she called back. "We're here."

"Geraldine!" he exclaimed. "You climbed the tree!"

"Yeah," she said, flushing.

"I didn't think she'd do it," Dub said. "But she did."

"Way to go," said Sam. Kizzy nudged his hand. He scratched her behind the ears. "Mind if I come up?" he asked.

"Come on," said Dub, and in the blink of an eye, it seemed, Sam was beside them.

"How'd you know where we were?" Dub asked.

Sam smiled. "Just a feeling. Your parents were about to form a search party. I told them I was on my way to look you up, anyhow." He paused, then said, "I came to say goodbye."

"You're leaving?" Geraldine asked. "So soon?"

"They're still picketing at Columbia—there's a guy

I met in Washington, asked me if I could help out. I have to go, Geraldine. But I'll be back soon—and off and on all summer. I'll always come back."

Geraldine's throat ached. She made a joke, to cover it. "Do you swear by the sacred tree?"

Sam put out his hand and touched their old initials. "I swear by the sacred Lover's Tree, eternal friendship and everlasting loyalty. . . ." He stopped.

"All for one, and one for all," Geraldine finished for him.

"Here, Captain," Sam said after a moment. He checked his pockets and handed Dub a small knife. "Time for some new initials."

Dub looked at Geraldine. They ought to be heading home pretty soon, she knew. Mama and Daddy would be waiting. But Sam was right. She nodded at her brother. "There's time," she said.

"Forever and ever," he said under his breath, and he began carving.